Willmott Dixon

The Jacobite Episode in Scottish history and its relative literature

Willmott Dixon

The Jacobite Episode in Scottish history and its relative literature

ISBN/EAN: 9783337204495

Printed in Europe, USA, Canada, Australia, Japan

Cover: Foto ©Andreas Hilbeck / pixelio.de

More available books at **www.hansebooks.com**

ESSAYS.

Glasgow Saint Andrew Society.

1874.

P<small>RINTED BY</small> W<small>ILLIAM</small> R<small>ANKIN</small>, 192 A<small>RGYLE</small> S<small>TREET</small>, G<small>LASGOW</small>.

UNDER the conditions of this year's Competition, Prizes fell to be awarded for the two best Essays. Twenty in all were presented, from various quarters, Scotland, England, and the Colonies. The task of making a selection was one of no small difficulty, partly, among other causes, owing to the conflicting partialities of the writers. In this respect, however, the Adjudicators did not feel either entitled, or called upon, to adopt the impressions, or indorse the animadversions of particular Essayists; but rather to discriminate fairly between the merits of the Essays, as combined historical and literary productions. The two selected will be found to differ widely from each other in the views maintained; but they thus afford an opportunity of seeing both sides of the historical picture.

G. FYFFE CHRISTIE,
President.

GLASGOW, October, 1874.

THE

Jacobite Episode in Scottish History

AND

ITS RELATIVE LITERATURE.

AN ESSAY

BY

WILLMOTT DIXON, LL. B.,

OF TRINITY COLLEGE, CAMBRIDGE, AND OF THE INNER
TEMPLE, BARRISTER-AT-LAW.

" Nor wanted at their end
.........................from tender hearts,
And those who sorrowed o'er a vanished race,
Pity, the violet on the tyrant's grave."—*Tennyson.   Aylmer's Field.*

JOHN MENZIES & COMPANY,
EDINBURGH & GLASGOW.

SIMPKIN, MARSHALL, & COMPANY,
LONDON.

PREFATORY NOTE.

As the limits of the present Essay do not admit of its being encumbered with copious references to authorities, the author thinks it desirable to give the following list of works consulted in its compilation:—

Memoirs of Lochiel—Correspondence of Colonel Hooke —Jacobite Correspondence of the Athole Family—The Lockhart Papers—The Culloden Papers—Memoirs of the Master of Sinclair—Memoirs of the Master of Lovat— Dalrymple's Memoirs of Great Britain and Ireland—Wodrow's Correspondence—Defoe's History of the Union—The Letters of Captain Burt—Macpherson's Original Papers— Patten's History of 1715—Rae's History of 1715—Forbes's Jacobite Memoirs of 1745—The Chevalier Johnstone's Memoirs of 1745—Genuine Memoirs of John Murray of Broughton—Dr. King's Political Anecdotes—Marchant's History of 1745—Henderson's ditto—Boyse's ditto—Home's ditto.

In addition to these contemporary records of the Jacobite Episode, the author has to express his indebtedness to the following later works:—

Thomson's Memoirs of the Jacobites—Jesse's Memoirs of the Pretenders — Oliphant's Jacobite Lairds of Gask —

Napier's Memorials of the Life and Times of Graham of Claverhouse—The Waverley Novels—Tales of a Grandfather—Chambers' History of 1745—Gregory's History of the Western Highlands—Brown's History of the Highlands—Wright's History of Scotland—Burton's History of Scotland from the Revolution—Lord Russell's Memoirs of the Affairs of Europe from the Peace of Utrecht—Buckle's History of Civilization—and the Histories of Hume, Mahon, and Macaulay.

With reference to the Ballad Literature of Jacobitism, the author has consulted the Collections of Hogg, Ritson, Cromek, Cunninghame, and Mackay.

THE

Jacobite Episode in Scottish History

AND ITS

RELATIVE LITERATURE..

" Tros Tyriusve mihi nullo discrimine agetur."—VIRGIL, Æn. 1, 574.

ROMANCE seems to have claimed the Jacobite Episode as its own, and has so fiercely resented any encroachment upon its domains that History has abandoned the field in despair. Even sober students, who have approached the subject with an honest desire for truthful inquiry and impartial investigation, have been unable to resist the magic spell, and have found themselves converted, against their will, from historians into romancers. They have seen every person and every circumstance connected with this episode through a glowing atmosphere of romance; and traditions which would, under ordinary conditions, have been scouted as poetical myths, have in this case been accepted as grave and indisputable historical facts.

But romance is not the only obstacle in the way of the patient and honest seeker after truth in this period of Scottish history. Another and almost as formidable an impediment is partizanship. Even now it is difficult to approach the subject without feeling something of party heat and something of party bias. What it must have been when personal recollections and experiences added tenfold bitterness to these feelings, is not hard to imagine. It was almost impossible for writers to take any middle course between the extremes of rabid Jacobitism and equally rabid Whiggism. And it is a wearisome task wading through the pages of extravagant eulogy or unmeasured invective, according as the writer treats of friends or enemies, which deface and obscure almost every record of this interesting and eventful period.

To the Jacobite, the inhabitants who peopled Great Britain at that time were divided into two classes—the angels who followed the exiled Stuarts, paragons of perfection, models of all that is chivalrous, noble, and heroic—and the devils who held by the usurping Elector of Hanover, monsters of iniquity and cruelty, poltroons, knaves, and scoundrels of the deepest dye. And, *mutatis mutandis*, the same holds true of the Whig. There is no believing or trusting either of them ; and all that the honest historical student can do, is to follow Ovid's advice, "*Medio tutissimus ibis*," and hope that a middle course will be nearer the truth than either extreme. It is in this spirit that I have essayed to treat the subject. If I have not always been able to free myself from the bias of political opinions, I have at least tried in the main to be impartial and give each side a fair hearing. That it is not always easy even to do this, all who have studied the subject will admit ; and they will bear me out, I am sure, in the assertion that the exasperating disregard of truth, the reckless acceptance of tradition, and the irrational love of romance, which are the chief characteristics of most of the literature of the Jacobite episode in Scottish history, are a sore trial of human patience.

With this explanation of the aim of the present essay, by way of preface, I shall proceed to sketch briefly the history of the Jacobite episode, dwelling chiefly on the causes which enabled Jacobitism to retain so tenacious a hold upon Scotland, reviewing some of the more prominent of its social and political results, and touching upon the literature, both contemporary and subsequent, which it produced, and the influence which that literature exercised over the sentiments of the Scottish people.

THE Revolution of 1688 was, on the whole, a quiet and orderly affair in England; men's passions were not much excited; the flight of one king and the arrival of another were facts accepted, to all outward appearance, with philosophical calmness, not to say indifference, by the large bulk of Englishmen. But it was far otherwise in Scotland. A long course of wanton and cruel persecution, of systematic tyranny and organised oppression, had kindled feelings of bitter hatred and resentment. The Scotch had seen their national Church, dear to them as their own lives, dishonoured and despoiled; whilst a Church which they hated and abhorred, a Church associated in their minds with all that was idolatrous, tyrannical, and odious, had been forced upon them by sword and fire, by the rack and the thumb-screw. They had seen hordes of savage Highlanders brought down from their mountain glens, at the express command of their sovereign, and quartered upon the inhabitants of those Western shires who had fought so heroically for the faith delivered to them by their fathers; they had witnessed the barbarous outrages and excesses which these ferocious mercenaries had committed, in pursuance of the

royal orders to devastate the country and harry
the people.   They had felt the intolerable in-
solence, arrogance, and injustice of the Bishops
whom the Crown had set over them as legisla-
tors, councillors, and judges—creatures who lent
themselves to every scheme for crushing civil
and religious liberty—creatures swoln with pride
and eaten up with avarice, who arrogated to
themselves all temporal as well as all spiritual
power.   With such grievances and sufferings
rankling in their memories, there can be little
wonder that the Scottish people hated Episcopacy with a deep and passionate hatred—a
hatred which the King to whom they owed it
shared equally with his Bishops.   They had no
grateful recollections of the Stuarts.   James I.,
Charles I., Charles II., had all done their fair
share towards laying up a legacy of hatred for
their line; but it was left to James II. to eclipse
all the iniquities of his predecessors.   The
most bloody and remorseless persecutor these
islands have ever seen, his barbarities towards

the hunted Covenanters were only matched by the atrocities of Philip II. in the Netherlands. For James personally enjoyed the spectacle of human suffering; it was a pleasure to him to witness the infliction of the most horrible tortures. And he had not even Philip's poor excuse—religious zeal; for these cruelties were perpetrated in behalf of a religion which in his secret soul he really hated as much as that he was persecuting. If English Protestants would but candidly and honestly study the records of Episcopal persecution in Scotland under the Stuarts, they would, perhaps, be less bitter in their invectives against Roman Catholic persecutors—they would certainly understand better the feelings with which the Scottish nation then regarded Episcopacy, and the deep - rooted national aversion to it which has shown itself so often since.

From the moment of James the Second's accession till his flight in 1688, Scotland had been subjected to a tyranny so cruel and so exhausting that, as Buckle truly remarks,* it would have broken the energy of almost any other nation. But, tough as their own mountain ash, the energy of Scotsmen is not to be easily broken. And the moment that the news of James's flight reached Scotland, the people seemed to spring into life again, like a twig which, long bent back, is at last loosed. They felt the spirit of liberty surging in their veins again, and with the memory of all that they had suffered under the tyrant fresh upon them, it was not likely that they would welcome such an event without feelings of intense excitement.

Under the influence of these feelings the Convention of the Estates of Scotland met on the 4th of April, 1689, and declared that James "hath forefaulted the right to the Crown, and the throne is become vacant." There was no legal fiction of abdication here, but a bold, blunt, outspoken statement of facts which contrasts favourably with the slavish and superstitious

---

* History of Civilization, vol. iii. chap. xxii.

reverence for precedent which marked the actions of the English Parliament, a feature of English parliamentary procedure which however safe and useful in the abstract, as a check upon rash and reckless innovations, has been often carried, as in this case, to absurd and unreasonable lengths. And this manly expression of opinion was the more creditable to the Scottish Parliament because it was attended with no little personal risk to those who uttered it. For Dundee's dragoons were clanking through the streets, and the Parliament House was within easy range of the guns of the Castle which the "Gay Gordon" still held for the fugitive monarch. The two hostile factions were in much more immediate danger of collision than in England. But the vote was passed without any actual display of violence, and James Stuart ceased to be King of Scotland as he had already ceased to be King of England.

There can be no question that the Revolution was welcomed with sincere and hearty joy by the great mass of the Scottish people. They had good reason to be joyful for such a signal deliverance from the clutches of the worst tyrant that had ever scourged their country. If there was any sympathy at all for James in Scotland at this time, it was a very lukewarm feeling, and even in that form only existed among those fanatical cavaliers with whom loyalty to the House of Stuart was a family heir-loom, the value of which they never dreamt of appraising, but were content to accept it on the strength of tradition, and cherish it with the unquestioning faith of children. The wrongs inflicted by the Stuarts had been too glaring to admit of any extenuation, and they were too fresh in the memories of all to allow of any feeling but that gratitude for the timely relief, which was uppermost in men's minds. How then did it come to pass that Scotland, which had more reason to detest the Stuart dynasty than any other part of the British Isles, and which welcomed the dethronement of that dynasty with

such unequivocal signs of gladness and enthusiasm, should of all other countries have
become, *par excellence*, the refuge and home of
Jacobitism ? What produced this extraordinary
revulsion of feeling ? Was it really a national
reaction, or was it merely the movement of a
bold and clamorous minority, composed of disappointed statesmen, selfish politicians, and a
few fanatical enthusiasts ? These are the questions which I shall endeavour to answer as fully
as the limited space at my disposal will allow.

After the Vote of Forfeiture had been passed
by the Scottish Parliament, the prospects of the
House of Stuart in Scotland were certainly not
encouraging, but they were not so utterly desperate as at first sight they may have appeared.
Of all the Scottish nobles, indeed, only three
remained faithful to James, but it must not
therefore be supposed that all the rest were
staunch supporters of the Revolution. Far from
it ; to quote the words of Sir John Dalrymple,*

* Memoirs of Great Britain and Ireland.

they merely "waited for events in hopes and fears from the old Government and the new, intriguing with both, and depended upon by neither." And the three faithful nobles really represented a far more certain and reliable source of strength and trust, than the crowd of wavering time-servers. These three were the nucleus of the future Jacobite party, and they were, the Duke of Gordon, Lord Balcarras, and Viscount Dundee. The two first played but a secondary and inconsiderable part in the events which followed, but the third was the great central figure of the first Jacobite rising, the life and soul and hope of Scottish Jacobitism. But for him William of Orange would have been peaceably proclaimed King of Scotland, and neither hand nor voice would have been raised in defence of James Stuart. Indeed, it is not too much to say, that it was only the bold and energetic action of Dundee at this critical moment which kept Jacobitism from expiring in Scotland, and made the rebellions of 1715 and 1745 possible.

Dundee was not a man of original genius, but he was gifted with a keen perception of the right thing to be done at the right moment, and with the necessary resolution and force of character to carry out promptly his conceptions. He was an ardent and devoted admirer of Montrose, whom, in many respects, he resembled, though far inferior both in moral and intellectual qualities to the great Marquis; and it was the success of that brilliant general at the head of an army of Highlanders, which suggested to Dundee the possibility of effecting a diversion in favour of his royal master at this juncture, by an attempt to raise the Highlands in revolt.

That "lying spirit" of romance, which is responsible for so much gross perversion of history, for so many false notions and deplorable misconceptions, has foisted upon the world no falsehood that has obtained wider credence than the famous fiction of Highland loyalty to the Stuarts. We have been taught to believe that these Highlanders, from the day they fought under Montrose, at Kilsyth, till the day they fought under Murray, at Culloden, were the staunch and devoted adherents, the leal and loyal henchmen of the House of Stuart, and the sturdy champions of divine right and hereditary succession. It is a picturesque and captivating idea; but unfortunately for those who have grounded upon it conclusions favourable to the Highland clans, it has no foundation whatever in fact. The Highlanders cared as little for the House of Stuart as for the House of Orange. What little they knew of the Stuarts by experience, was not calculated to increase their affection and respect for that dynasty. James VI. had coolly planned their extermination, his successors had indorsed the scheme, and it was not from any want of vigorous efforts to carry it into execution that it had failed. Of James VII., indeed, they had some more pleasurable recollections, for he had on one or two occasions made them the instruments of his vengeance upon the Covenanters, and they were naturally grateful for the opportunity of gratifying with impunity, not only their predatory inclinations, but also their revenge upon the despised and detested Lowlanders, between whom and themselves there had existed a deadly feud and deep-rooted hatred for centuries. But beyond this the Highlanders had no reason whatever to cherish any feelings of gratitude or affection for the Stuarts, whose laws they had persistently defied, and whose heavy chastisements they had frequently suffered. To assert that there was any innate loyalty to the Stuart family among the Highlanders is simply to betray sheer ignorance of their habits, their customs, and their internal government. They owned no authority, they recognized no sovereignty but that of the chief of the clan; him they were bound to follow in whatever enterprize he engaged. Whatever side in a quarrel their chief, from policy or inclination, chose to take, for that side they were bound to fight without asking any questions; for it was to the chief only that they owed allegiance; and not one of them but would have felt it the deadliest insult to be told that he was a subject of any other king in Christendom. The predilections of the chiefs were invariably in favour of the side which offered most opportunities for plunder and revenge. They were at this time a race of brawlers, murderers, and robbers, without any of those chivalrous feelings which were claimed for them at a later date, and which were unquestionably developed as they advanced in civilization. Fletcher of Saltoun who, like all genuine Scotchmen of his day, despised and abhorred the Highlanders as a race of worthless freebooters who were a disgrace to the country, thus pithily sums up his estimate of them—" A people who are all gentlemen only because they will not work ; and who in everything are more contemptible than the vilest slaves, except that they always carry arms, because for the most part they live on robbery."

At this early stage of the Jacobite movement the leaders of the clans played fast and loose with both sides; and it was not until some rash or careless step had irretrievably compromised him, that a chief definitely took sides with either party. There was very little romantic sentiment about the Highland chief. He possessed a large share of the national shrewdness, he knew how to make a good bargain, and had a keen eye to the main chance. He must be persuaded that the advantage to be gained by espousing the cause of King James, was decidedly greater than that to be gained by espousing the cause of King William, before he would budge a step or strike a blow for the exiled monarch. But once the chief was gained, the clan followed as a matter of course; they had no choice; the chief settled for which cause they were to fight; it was not for them either to dispute his commands or inquire into his motives; with the preliminary negotiations they did not concern themselves, their business was to obey the order of their chief,

and fight just when and for whom he pleased.*
When Dundee, therefore, resolved to set out
and rouse the Highlands to arms, it was not
because he expected to find more loyalty there
than in the Lowlands, but because he knew that
the clans were always ready for fighting and
plunder, and might therefore be more easily
and rapidly collected for a sudden movement.
Dundee had sufficient tact and eloquence to
induce the chiefs to associate the cause of the
Stuarts, (which simply on its own merits they
would have regarded with indifference,) with all
that they loved best—revenge upon the clans
they hated, and a raid upon the Lowlands. On
these conditions they were ready to forget certain passages in their former relations with the
Stuarts—they had a bond of union and sympathy now in their common hatred of the existing

---

* A curious illustration of this feature of the clan system is to be found
in the conduct of the Fraser clan. In 1715, they fought on the Hanoverian
side, because at that time it suited the interests of their chief, the notorious
Simon, Lord Lovat, to take that side. In 1745, they fought on the Jacobite
side, because their wily and fickle leader saw fit to change his mind.

government, which, whether Stuart or Orange, was to the Highlander always odious as the representative of law, order, and justice, three abstractions which he cordially detested.

But the Highlanders, as the most prominent actors in the Jacobite episode, have not only been credited with a loyalty which they neither understood nor professed, they have also been credited most unjustly with all the prowess which has made Scotland renowned for centuries as a martial nation. Everywhere outside Scotland, Highlander and Scot have been taken as synonymous terms; and, even now, I question whether a very large section of Englishmen do not make the same confusion, and, because there is no very palpable line of demarcation at this day between Highlands and Lowlands, conclude that all inhabitants of Scotland, from the Solway to the Orkneys, are and always have been of the same race; and that the great martial exploits of Scottish history have all been achieved by the ancestors of those kilted heroes who beat Cope at Prestonpans and routed Hawley at Falkirk. Ignorant romancers have fostered this delusion by pictures of Bruce and Wallace, in kilt and tartan, at the head of their plaided clansmen, which, letting alone the fact that neither kilt nor tartan existed till some two centuries later,* is as absurd an anomaly, to borrow Macaulay's illustration, as to represent George Washington, in his character of leader of the Americans, brandishing a tomahawk and girt with a string of scalps. The Highlanders were of a totally

---

* It has been the fashion to speak of the kilt or philabeg as the ancient national dress of the Highlanders. Few, perhaps, are aware that the kilt, as we now know it, is not of Scottish origin at all. The honour of its invention is divided between two Englishmen—an army tailor who accompanied Marshal Wade's force to Scotland in 1719, and Thomas Rawlinson, overseer of some iron-works in Glengarry's country. For more than a century previous to this the tartan plaid had been the common garb of the Highlanders, but it was all in one piece, wound in folds round the body, leaving the knees bare. It was worn in much the same way as the Red Indian now wears his blanket -- its appearance was equally grotesque, and its condition equally filthy. English people in 1715 and 1745 were horrified at the disgusting and revolting appearance of the Highlanders, with their matted hair and beards, their unwashed skins, and their greasy, vermin-covered blankets of tartan, their only article of attire. Previous to the adoption of the tartan, which probably took place about the close of the fifteenth century, the long loose saffron-coloured shirt was the Highland garb.

different race from those steel-clad spearmen of the dales, whom Bruce and Wallace led to victory—before whose disciplined valour and serried phalanx, the despised Highland savages were scattered like chaff. The famous Scottish heroes were Lowlanders, little if at all different in race, manners, and speech, from their English neighbours. Bruce himself was an English baron, bred if not born in England; his father was an English courtier, his grandfather an English judge,—and he would have scorned any connection with the savage kernes of the Highlands, who were never admitted to be Scots. In behalf of the Lowlanders who have made Scotland what she is, and to whom of right belongs the glory of her ancient prowess, I think it is but fair to restore to them the credit which the Highlanders, as the heroes of the Jacobite rebellions, have usurped. It does not in any way detract from the reputation of the Highlanders for valour—a reputation nobly won and as nobly maintained. But the Highlanders' renown dates no farther back than the time of Montrose, while that of the Lowlanders can be proudly traced back to Bannockburn, and far beyond, till it is lost in the mists of tradition.

In speaking of the spirit and sentiments of the Highland chiefs when they joined Dundee in 1689, I do not mean to assert that these were the feelings which actuated them all through the Jacobite episode. No doubt fifty years worked a considerable change both in the sentiments and the manners of the Highlanders, and many of them entered upon the rebellion of 1745 from other motives than those I have described. On this point I shall have occasion to speak in its proper place, but enough has been said here to show that loyalty to the House of Stuart was certainly not the motive which led the clans to take arms under Dundee.

It is a proof of Dundee's remarkable sagacity and tact, that he, a Lowlander by birth and breeding, a stranger and of a hated race, wholly ignorant of the language and manners of these wild mountaineers, should have succeeded in gathering round himself all their military enthusiasm, and have persuaded them to accept him as their leader. The very fact, however, of his being a stranger gave him one great advantage —no clan felt aggrieved at serving under him, no chief considered his dignity compromised, as he would unquestionably have done had any Highland chieftain, no matter what his rank or power, attempted to take the command. The rivalry of the various clans was carried to the most absurd extremes; there was as much jealousy and sensitiveness among them on points of precedence and etiquette, as among the court ladies of Louis Quatorze. Dundee's tact was invaluable in reconciling the differences which arose from these petty rivalries, differences which threatened a hundred times to turn the swords of one half of his army against the other half. This little resolute dark man, " Black John of the Battles," as they loved to call him, with the face so melancholy and beautiful in repose, so stern and cruel when roused to action, had an influence over them which they themselves felt to have something weird and uncanny about it. They regarded him with a strange mixture of admiration and superstitious awe. There is something in the commanding intellect of a little man which always has this effect upon brute force, and it is a noteworthy fact that the greatest generals the world has seen have been of the same physical type, and have in consequence wielded the same moral influence. That Dundee should have kept together an army composed of such discordant elements and such inflammable materials for a single week, is a wonder which increases our admiration of his tact the more we study it; but that even he, with all his tact and cleverness, could have kept such an army together long enough to do any real or lasting service to the House of Stuart, is more than we can believe possible. It would have melted away from him as a similar army had melted away from Montrose, even in the hour of his triumph. And even supposing it had not been so; supposing all the great results, which Dundee's sanguine admirers believed would have ensued but for the abrupt close of his career, had actually come to pass—what would the Stuarts have done with these victorious Highlanders? How could they have shown their gratitude to these lawless warriors, with due regard to the safety and order of their kingdom and the security of their law-loving lieges? They would have found these wild and reckless freebooters a terrible thorn in their side; they would have been compelled at last to put down their excesses with a strong and stern hand; and it would have been worse for the Highlanders in the end, perhaps, than Culloden.

Dundee, however, kept his Highland army together long enough to immortalize his own name, and shed a ray of sentiment over the field of Killiecrankie, which did more for Jacobitism than the victory itself, for it gave it a memory which in days to come was a sure spell to conjure up Highland enthusiasm. The victory itself, indeed, was not a brilliant one; and the success, such as it was, must be attributed to the impetuous rush of the clans, rather than to the skilful dispositions of the general. But Dundee gained that spurious fame which attaches to death on the field of battle, and which is supposed to be the highest glory that can crown a soldier's career. It is hard to tell why it should be so—in this case especially hard—for the circumstances of Dundee's death were rather ignominiqus than otherwise. And yet while the cool and steady courage and splendid retreat of Mackay are forgotten, the accident which gave Dundee the honour of his death-wound will be remembered as though it had been some noble achievement of his own.

Of the character of Dundee it is not easy to form a correct estimate. That he was a soldier and a gentleman, a chivalrous and devoted cavalier, I think there is good reason to believe; but it is equally true that with these qualities

were combined the hardness, the selfishness, and
the recklessness of human life, which were the
results, partly of a naturally stern disposition,
partly of long training as a mercenary in continental camps.   Probably one half of the tales
told by the Covenanters of his cruelty are either
exaggerated or wholly untrue; but even making
due allowance for the rabid hostility and fanatical
hatred of the Covenanters, whose malignant and
persistent efforts to blacken his character by fair
means and foul have done their cause more
harm than good, his own letters show that there
are abundant grounds for the stigma of merciless
and cold-blooded cruelty which rests upon his
name.   Many chivalrous efforts have been made
to cleanse his memory from these dark stains,*

---

* Macaulay's strictures on Dundee have called forth three doughty champions.   Professor Aytoun in a special note attached to his "Lays of the
Scottish Cavaliers," Mr. John Paget in his "New Examen," Mr. Mark
Napier in his "Memorials of the Life and Times of John Graham of Claverhouse," have all striven hard to clear the fame of their hero; and a greater
than any of them has also taken up the cudgels in his behalf, though for
dramatic effect he once joined the other side.   In a letter from Scott to
Southey there occurs this curious passage in reference to Dundee: "As for

but I confess that all the eloquence and all the arguments of his champions seem to me to have failed to establish his innocence, although to some extent they may have cleared his fame. But while it is impossible to believe that he was either the fiend that his fanatical enemies paint him, or the Christian hero that his equally fanatical admirers represent him, I think we may fairly say of him, that with all his faults, and they were neither few nor small, he had most of the virtues of a cavalier of the best type; and the cause of the exiled Stuarts, from first to last, numbered among its followers none abler, more gallant, or more devoted than John Graham of Claverhouse.

---

my good friend, Dundee, I cannot admit his culpability in the extent you allege; and it is scandalous of the Sunday bard (Wordsworth) to join in your condemnation, 'and yet come of a noble Graeme'! I admit he was *tant soit peu sauvage*, but he was a noble savage; and the *beastly Covenanters*, against whom he acted, hardly had any claim to be called men, unless what was founded on their walking upon their hind feet. You can hardly conceive the perfidy, cruelty, and stupidity of these people, according to the accounts they have themselves preserved." This is not quite in harmony with the sentiments expressed in "Old Mortality," but Scott himself admitted that he was in that instance carried away by his subject.

With the death of Dundee at Killiecrankie the first Jacobite rising may be said to have virtually ended.   But before it actually closed it was marked by one brilliant exploit on the other side which it would be unfair to pass over in silence. The memorable defence of Dunkeld by the Cameronians stands unequalled as a military achievement in all the annals of the Jacobite wars. They had been left in this lonely and unfortified outpost, as they believed, from the same motive which led Joab to place Uriah the Hittite in the forefront of the battle.   But so far from murmuring, they accepted the desperate situation with grim delight.   The same stern Puritan spirit which had turned Marston Moor from a defeat into a victory was here.   It rose to fever heat as one avenue of escape after another was closed.   The more hopeless their position became, the higher rose the fierce fanatical joy of battle.   For hours they held their own against tenfold odds, until, repulsed at all points, the Highlanders fled in confusion.   But the victory was dearly bought; the gallant young leader of the Cameronians, William Cleland, who, had he lived, would have rivalled the fame of Dundee, was shot dead while stimulating his men by his own noble example to prolong what seemed a hopeless struggle, a death more glorious and heroic than the great Jacobite leader's, though it has found no *sacer vates* to give it a niche in the temple of fame.

The ridiculous stampede of Cromdale, when the Highlanders ran like sheep, and the Jacobite generals only escaped capture by flying in ignominious *déshabille*, the one without hat, coat, or sword, the other in literally nothing but his night-gown, brought to a close a war of which the Jacobites had little reason to be proud.

William and his advisers were not slow to read the lessons taught by this first Jacobite rising. They saw that the Highlanders were ready to take up arms at the beck and call of any party who would promise them plunder and pay, and that they would therefore be a perpetual source of danger and anxiety to the Revolution Government if left open to the overtures of the Jacobites. Had William been unfettered by foreign complications, he would probably have subjugated the Highlands at the point of the sword, but he had other and more urgent work for his army, and he was anxious, therefore, to get the Highlanders off his hands as soon as possible. Pacific measures promised the speediest solution of the difficulty. Efforts were accordingly made to gain over the chiefs, and the direction which those efforts took showed how low an opinion William held of Scottish morality. Indeed, when dealing with Scotchmen, whether Lowlanders or Highlanders, William always acted on the principle that a bribe was the best argument to convince a Scottish under-standing.* In his instructions to Lord Melville

* He was not alone in his opinion of the venality of Scotchmen. Col. Hooke, who was sent over by Lonis XIV., in 1705, to sound the Scottish Jacobites, thus described them to his royal master:—"Les Ecossais sont pauvres et ils aiment l'argent ; une somme considerable répandue à propos gagnera les chefs." And again :—"Ç'est une maxime en Ecosse de ne point

as his High Commissioner in Scotland, he openly countenanced, and not only countenanced, but distinctly recommended a wholesale system of bribery, and gave minute directions to buy off leading men of the opposition with the offer of state appointments or presents of money. There was, no doubt, much in the conduct and character of the influential Scotch nobles and politicians of that time to warrant his holding such an opinion. But William did not understand the Scotch character; he did not take into account the fact that their pride was stronger even than their venality, and that nothing could be more offensive to that pride than the blunt and business-like way in which these dishonourable proposals were conveyed. Many of the most grievous mistakes in the policy both of William and of his successors towards Scotland are to be attributed to this ignorance of the national character of the Scotch.

perdre son poste lorsque l'on peut conserver quand le diable viendrois." Not very complimentary to the Scotch; but then, Colonel Hooke was himself a renegade Scotchman, and that may account for his bitterness.

It was resolved, therefore, to bribe the Highland chiefs, and the Earl of Breadalbane was
entrusted with £20,000 for that purpose, with
directions to offer £2,000 or a dignity under an
earldom to any chief whose allegiance it might
be necessary to purchase at so high a price.
Breadalbane, who, if we are to believe one of
his contemporaries,* was " cunning as a fox, wise
as a serpent, but slippery as an eel," was
strongly suspected of embezzling the larger portion of this sum, and making threats and promises
serve the purpose of bribes among the Highland
chiefs. It is certain that he gave no account of
his disbursements; and to all inquiries answered
coolly "the money is spent, the Highlands are
quiet, and this is the only way of accounting
among friends."

Not satisfied, however, with Breadalbane's
assurance of the loyal and peaceful disposition
of the Highlanders, the Government issued a
proclamation summoning all chiefs to take the

---

* Memoirs of the Secret Services of John Macky.

C

oath of allegiance before January 1st, 1692, on pain of having " letters of fire and sword " issued against them. Abundant time was allowed for complying with the terms of the proclamation. But many of the chiefs delayed their submission as long as possible, in the hope that something might occur to obviate the necessity of an act so inimical to their marauding instincts and love of independence. The most dilatory of all these was the crafty old chief of Glencoe, who, in the expectation of a fresh Jacobite movement, put off taking the oath until it was too late to do so within the appointed time. The story of what followed is too well known to need repetition here. That it was the intention of William and his ministers to make a signal example of any who should fail to comply with the strict terms of the proclamation, there can be no doubt. It is equally certain that there was a general wish, in which William participated,* that some of the

* In a letter from the Earl of Linlithgow to Breadalbane, published for the first time in the *Edinburgh Review*, No. 213, there occurs this remarkable

most obstinate clans would hold out, in order
that the tremendous punishment inflicted on
them might overawe the rest of the Highlands,
and render it unnecessary to keep a large force
there any longer. This was the broad and
general view of the matter taken by William and
his English ministers. But besides this, there
was an under-current of local jealousy and irritation at work, and some plausible excuse was
wanted by Breadalbane, Dalrymple, and others,
for rooting out the Macdonalds of Glencoe, who
were regarded by their Lowland neighbours
with much the same feelings as those with which
the settlers in Oregon regard the Modoc Indians.
Indeed the action of William and his advisers,
and more especially of Sir John Dalrymple,
cannot be better understood than by calling to
mind recent[*] events in America. Long before
the massacre which led to General Grant's edict

and significant passage:—" But the last standers out may pay for all; and
*besides, I know that the K—— does not care that some do it, that he may make examples
of them.*"

 * This was written in the Spring of 1873.

of extermination against the Modocs, there were men of high reputation—men like General Sheridan, who warmly maintained that the only safe and prudent policy to pursue towards the Indians was a policy of extermination. And this was the opinion of all who had any experi-ence of the Indians on the borders of the far Western settlements. Yet no one accuses General Sheridan of any private or personal enmity against " Captain Jack," in persistently advocating that ruthless policy—and no one accuses President Grant of gross inhumanity in finally adopting that policy after the massacre of General Canby and his fellow-commissioners. And it seems to me just as unreasonable to accuse Sir John Dalrymple of personal enmity against Glencoe, or William of barbarous in-humanity, because the one advocated, and the other approved of a scheme to inflict signal chastisement upon a gang of mountain-robbers. With Dalrymple, it was a sincere belief that to exterminate these Highland caterans was the only means of securing the peace and safety of their Lowland neighbours. We find him in his letters seriously and calmly arguing the matter from this point of view. "I believe," he says, on one occasion, "that you will be satisfied it were a great advantage to the nation that thieving tribe were rooted out and cut off." This was no new sentiment. It can be traced through the policy of all the later Scottish kings, and it was a source of mortification and vexation to them that they were unable to carry it thoroughly into execution. James VI., who, whatever his faults, has never been accused of inhumanity, actually entered into a contract "to extirpate that barbarous people." It was a traditional feature in Scottish policy, and there is therefore nothing surprising in finding it advocated by Dalrymple. As for William, he was too cold-blooded to care much by what means a measure of expediency was carried out. Of Glencoe's tardy submission, he probably knew nothing; of the base treachery of the catastrophe he is guiltless; but that he knew what his advisers meant by "extirpating" a clan, when he put that unrestricted warrant into their hands, the preceding contemporaneous evidence leaves us no room to doubt. The responsibility of the hideous and revolting details rests solely with the executioners; and those whose admiration of Highland virtue amounts to a species of fetichism, will do well to bear in mind that this foul deed of treachery and murder was perpetrated *by Highlanders,* and in accordance with a custom for which Highland annals afford no lack of precedents.*

At the same time there is good reason to doubt whether we should ever have heard much, if anything, of the Massacre of Glencoe, but for the Jacobites and the personal enemies of Dalrymple. To the former it was a godsend. They seized upon it with avidity. It offered

---

* For instances of the perfidy which Highlanders were not ashamed to avail themselves of in prosecuting their schemes of revenge, see an article in the *Quarterly Review,* No. 28 (vol. 14), the author of which is believed to have been Sir Walter Scott.

far too good a chance of vilifying their opponents to be neglected. It was paraded as a characteristic act of the new king—a foretaste of what his subjects might expect under his mild paternal rule. And so skilful was the use made of it, that William's government never succeeded in removing the odium which it brought upon them, whilst it was unquestionably of invaluable service to the Jacobite cause by lending it the moral support which it needed. Dalrymple's enemies, too, and they were many and powerful, made great capital out of this incident. They pounced upon it, and clung to it with all the tenacity of relentless malice. And there can be no doubt that personal hatred and jealousy of the Secretary of State, far more than any feelings of outraged humanity, were at the bottom of the popular agitation which brought about the subsequent investigation. The Massacre of Glencoe stands out prominently from other similar atrocities in Scottish history, not because it was more treacherous and inhuman, but because it happened at a time when it was peculiarly useful to a political party in the state, whose interest it was to make the most of anything which, by the force of rabid partisanship and unscrupulous ingenuity, could be made to blacken the characters of their opponents, and pave the way for their own restoration to popular favour.

The indignation aroused by the Massacre of Glencoe had hardly begun to subside, when there came the Darien Scheme, surely the wildest, most extravagant, and hopeless scheme in which a nation, proverbial for its caution and common sense, ever embarked. The story of its miserable failure, and the terrible sufferings of those hapless colonists left to perish on the lonely isthmus, is familiar to all students of Scottish history. For that failure England was, whether justly or unjustly it would be out of place to discuss here, held responsible, and feelings of the bitterest animosity were roused against the English Government. Everything that tended to alienate the two countries was advantageous to the cause of Jacobitism, and it was therefore only natural that the Jacobites should use every means at their disposal to foment the ill-feeling. The people of Scotland at this juncture were in much the same frame of mind as the shareholders of a company which has suddenly collapsed. They had lost their money, and they were fretful and angry, and disposed to believe the very worst that could be said of those to whom they attributed their loss. The general depression of trade consequent upon the failure of the Darien Scheme added fresh bitterness to these feelings, and produced such wide-spread discontent that on the death of Queen Mary the Government party were actually afraid, in the then temper of the Scottish Parliament, to bring forward the question of the Hanoverian succession, and that measure was in fact never passed by the Parliament of Scotland. This was one of the main reasons for the opposition of the Jacobites to the Act of Union. While Scotland was a separate kingdom, with a separate Parliament, they felt that they were strong enough to prevent the Act which extended the succession to the Electors of Hanover from being carried; and consequently on the death of Anne, James VIII. would be the only lawful King of Scotland; his claim would then be indisputable, because twofold; the merger of two distinct rights would give it double strength, for the crown would be his by the right of reversion, as well as by the right of hereditary descent. It is well to understand this clearly, because it gives the clue to the action of the Jacobites at this period.

It was while this discontent and irritation were still rankling in the hearts of the Scotch that the project for the Union of the two countries was first broached. It was not, indeed, a novel scheme; for more than a century it had been familiar to the thoughtful statesmen of both countries, and had been regarded as an event which must sooner or later take place, nor had it ever been received with disfavour by those who had contemplated its consummation. To William it had been one of the dearest wishes of his heart, and in his very last public utterance he earnestly commended it to the attention of the legislature in both countries. Nothing can be more certain than that the idea of Union in the abstract was not distasteful to the Scotch. But it was unfortunate that it should have been brought prominently forward at a time when the relations between the two countries were such as to strengthen the hands of its enemies and weaken the hands of its supporters.

The first negotiations for the Union were begun in 1702, but the vigorous opposition of the Jacobites rendered them unsuccessful. Three years later they were renewed, and in the interval the irritation and discontent of the Scotch had subsided in a very remarkable degree. This change, I think, may be attributed to the fact that there had been a lull in the Jacobite agitation, for it was that organised agitation alone which had kept Scotland in a state of ferment. The Jacobites had been quiet from policy. It was generally believed that Anne was in favour of her nephew's accession, and would, if not alarmed by any violent demonstrations on the part of James's adherents, exert all her influence to secure his succession to the throne. It was therefore the policy of the Jacobites not to make themselves obnoxiously prominent, and, owing to this policy, the land had rest, and the memory of old grievances began to fade. Consequently, when a proposal for the Union of the two countries was again mooted, the bulk of the people were prepared to accept it, and if they did not support the measure with enthusiasm, they at any rate viewed it with contentment. Nor is there any reason to doubt that this state of things would have continued, and that the Act of Union would have been passed without any excitement or violent display of feeling, had the Jacobites only preserved the passive attitude which they had of late assumed. But they were not sufficiently certain of Anne's support, nor sufficiently assured of its value to risk the passing of an Act of Union, the first result of which would be to make Scotland amenable to the laws of the English Parliament, and render the armies of England available for the defence of Scotland. The strength of the English Whigs would neutralize Jacobite influence in Scotland ; and, if the Act of Union were once passed, there would be no hope of preventing the Act securing the succession to the House of Hanover from being extended to Scotland. At all hazards, then, Scotland must be kept a separate kingdom, at any rate until the exiled Stuarts were again firmly re-established. It was with mingled rage and apprehension, therefore, that the Jacobites viewed the tame acquiescence of the great mass of the people in a measure which, if passed, must deal a deadly blow to Jacobitism. But they were determined that matters should not long remain in this state. Prompt and vigorous measures were taken to stir up the smouldering embers of half-forgotten wrongs, and revive the old hostility to England. They were utterly reckless what passions they inflamed, or what excesses they encouraged, so long as their immediate object was gained. Mischievous agitators laboured to exasperate the people against England. The memories of Glencoe and Darien were raked up, and England's share in them painted in the blackest colours. Every class of society, every profession, every trade was incited to oppose the Union by vehement assurances that the measure would be ruinous to the interests of each and all of them. All that the bitter invective and rancorous abuse, the artful and unscrupulous misrepresentation, the gross and persistent lying of hired lampooners and pamphleteers could do to alienate the Scotch from England, and exasperate them against the Union, was done. And knowing, as we do, how easily and with what little show of reason popular demonstrations are got up in our own day, there is surely nothing wonderful in the success which attended these efforts of the Jacobites. They unquestionably did, by the means I have described, create suspicion and dislike of the Union, and persuade the thoughtless and ignorant that the object of the measure was to sell Scotland to the English, and that, if they accepted it, their laws, liberties, and estates would for the future be at the disposal of an English Parliament.

And yet, after all these exertions, their success was only partial. Even when the agitation against the Union was at fever-heat, the nation was by no means unanimous in its dislike. The majority of the people were still in favour of the Union, though the minority were, as minorities generally are, the more noisy and demonstrative, making up in clamour for what they lacked in numbers. There is a passage in Burke's "Reflections on the Revolution in France," which is applicable to this as to most other popular agitations, it is this—" Because half a dozen grasshoppers under a fern make the field ring

with their importunate chink, whilst thousands
of great cattle, reposed beneath the shadow of
the British oak, chew the cud and are silent,
pray do not imagine that those who make the
noise are the only inhabitants of the field—that,
of course, they are many in number,—or, that,
after all, they are other than the little, shrivelled,
meagre, hopping, though loud and troublesome
insects of the hour."

The opposition to the Act of Union in
Scotland was, therefore, almost entirely the work
of the Jacobite party, who felt that their last
hold upon Scotland was slipping from them, and
that a desperate effort was necessary to keep it.
And when, in spite of all their efforts, the great
measure was passed, it was they who, out of
sheer spleen and spitefulness, fabricated and
circulated the foul calumny which attributed the
successful issue of the measure to the bribery of
the Scottish Ministers—a charge which, in an
age when political morality was at a low ebb,
was sure to find ready credence. There is

absolutely no valid evidence to support the charge, which rests mainly upon a list published in the papers of George Lockhart of Carnwath, a bitter and rabid Jacobite, who invariably imputes the worst motives to all who are not of his way of thinking. This list purports to give the name of every Scotchman of importance who was thought worth bribing, with the amount paid to each by the English Government, and Lockhart asserts that it is a genuine document which accidentally fell into his hands. There is no reason to question the genuineness of the document; but the fallacy of the assumption which Lockhart founded upon it, has been ably and clearly exposed by a living historian,* the most impartial and trustworthy of all who have written on the Jacobite Episode. The moneys alluded to in this list were a loan of £20,000, requested and obtained from the English Exchequer by the Scottish Government, to pay arrears of salary due to officials, who were

* Burton, Vol. I., pp. 484-494.

inclined to be angry and discontented at the delay. The application of the money was rigidly investigated by that celebrated Tory Committee which ruined Marlborough and sent Walpole to the Tower, but, *they* did not find that the payments were misappropriated; and we may be sure that if there had been the slightest suspicion of bribery, they would have smelt it out, and fastened upon it remorselessly. Indeed, the list itself seems to me to contain the refutation of the charge which has been founded upon it, for it includes the names of some who were notorious opponents of the Union, and systematically voted against it. And besides, it is a slur upon the reputation of Scotchmen for shrewdness, to suppose that they would not have made better bargains for the sale of their honour and patriotism—that a nobleman like Lord Banff, for example, would have sold his honour, his country, and his religion to boot, for the ridiculous sum of £11 : 2s.! And yet such staunch Scotsmen as Sir Walter Scott, and

Mr. Robert Chambers, have accepted this reckless charge, and have preferred to believe a shameful calumny against their own countrymen, rather than forego the pleasure of indulging their scorn and hatred of the Whigs! A singular and melancholy instance of judgment warped by partisanship.

It was not until the Jacobites had tried every other expedient in vain, that, as a last resource, they turned to France, hoping that assistance from that quarter would enable them to strike a blow before the two kingdoms became actually united, and one government had control over the defence of both. Then commenced those intrigues between the Scottish Jacobites and the French Court, which raised so many sanguine hopes destined to end only in misery and despair. It is doubtful whether the French Court was ever sincere in its support of Jacobitism, or ever seriously desired its success. The cause of the exiled Stuarts was a safe card to play whenever it served the ends of French policy to distract, and harass, and perplex English statesmen, but I do not believe that any one of the expeditions to which the French government ostensibly gave its sanction was ever really intended to succeed, and the false encouragement which these successive feints imparted to the Jacobite cause was mainly instrumental in accelerating its ultimate ruin.

It has been often said that there never was a more favorable opportunity for a great Jacobite movement than at the time when the agitation against the Union was at its height. It has been asserted that Scotland would have risen *en masse* to welcome back her exiled King, and that the united efforts of English and Scottish Jacobites would have carried the white cockade in triumph to Whitehall. But this assertion is based, I think, upon the grand mistake which was made by the Jacobites all through the Jacobite episode, viz.: that irritation and discontent against England meant sympathy with Jacobitism. No doubt the Jacobites had by astute policy identified themselves with all the popular grievances, notably with this agitation against the Union, and had done something towards associating Jacobitism in the popular mind with the assertion of national rights and the preservation of national independence. They were so far successful that there was a great deal of Jacobitism *talked* in Scotland by indignant opponents of the Union, who, in the excitement of the moment, forgot all that they had suffered from the Stuart dynasty. But when it came to *acting*, it was quickly seen how hollow was the Jacobitism of such professors. At the prospect of an actual restoration of a family which they had too good reason to distrust and dislike, they took alarm at once, and there were no deeds forthcoming to back up the words spoken in moments of heated and generally vinous enthusiasm. Colonel Hooke, who was sent over by Louis XIV., in 1705, to sound the Scottish Jacobites, and report upon the prospects of Jacobitism in Scotland, has left the minutest details of his mission, and the whole tenour of his report is, that there was no earnestness or heart in the Jacobite movement in Scotland. He found the principal men backward and timid. The great Highland chiefs were uncommonly shy even of being interviewed on the subject of an armed rising, and absolutely averse to joining in any such enterprize. The eminent politicians and statesmen, to whom Colonel Hooke had been directed as the leaders of the party, he found wholly devoid of any real interest in Jacobitism, which they merely used as a political watchword to rally a party of opposition against their parliamentary rivals. There was no depth or sincerity in the great mass of Scottish Jacobitism. And there can be little doubt that the report which Colonel Hooke (who, as his published correspondence proves, was a shrewd and acute observer,) brought back to his royal master, caused Louis XIV. to distrust all the representations of Scottish Jacobites in the future, and to be cautious of compromising himself by lending them any material aid. The ultimate collapse of Jacobitism was due to false representations on both sides. The Scottish Jacobites were for ever sending to France exaggerated accounts of the favourable aspect of Jacobitism in Scotland, in the hope of inducing the French Court, on the strength of these reports, to fit out a powerful expedition for an immediate invasion; while the French Cabinet was for ever sending to Scotland assurances of speedy assistance, which had the effect of keeping the Jacobites in a perpetual state of excitement and anticipation, and which undoubtedly precipitated the rebellions of 1715 and 1745. Each side was trying to dupe the other—but, unfortunately for the Jacobites, they failed to dupe, and were duped instead. They believed the representations of the French Court, whereas the French Court was never for a moment deceived by theirs.

Another broken reed upon which the Scottish Jacobites leaned was the co-operation of the

English Jacobites. And it is really extraordinary how little pains they took to inform themselves correctly of the spirit and the sentiments of the Jacobite party in England. The two seem to have been playing at cross-purposes, and neither knew exactly what the other wanted. The Scottish Jacobites wanted a repeal of the Union, a national King, and a national Parliament ; and, to obtain these objects, they were not averse to a French invasion. The English Jacobites, on the other hand, were in favour of the Union, and desirous of seeing their hereditary sovereign rule over the united countries, under one and the same constitutional government, but nothing would have induced them to sanction a French invasion. They had, as Englishmen, an unconquerable aversion to the presence of a foreign soldiery in the country, and in the event of an invasion their patriotism would have proved too strong for their Jacobitism.* This variance of

* A notable example of this feeling was afforded by the conduct of Admiral Russell, at La Hogue ; the Englishman was stronger than the

aims and difference of sentiments were fatal to
any united and concerted action. And yet,
although no attempt seems ever to have been
made to effect a compromise between these two
sections of the same party, and render concerted
action possible, both in 1715 and 1745 the
Scottish Jacobites took it for granted, with the
most extraordinary infatuation, that they had
the full sympathy of the English Jacobites, and
that the active co-operation of the latter would
follow as a matter of course. How unfounded
these expectations were, the history of the expeditions into England in 1715 and 1745 clearly
proves. And in each case the complete disappointment of those expectations was such a
sudden and unlooked-for blow, that the enterprize
collapsed at once.

These seem to have been the main causes of
the utter failure of the Jacobite movement, and

Jacobite in that gallant sailor, when it came to the push ; and all his loyalty
to the House of Stuart could not make him forget that he was opposed to the
natural enemies of his country, and that his first duty was to retrieve her
tarnished laurels by avenging the defeat of Beechy Head.

they were causes which existed from the first, and might have been early removed had there been any wise and able men among the advisers of the House of Stuart. But there were none. And it speaks volumes against Jacobitism, that hardly a single able, sensible, practical man in either country was found among its supporters. Indeed, there seems to me to have been something amateurish about all the efforts of Jacobitism. They were the attempts of *dilettanti* insurrectionists, with no fixed plans and no definite ideas, enthusiasts without that hearty practicality which can alone make enthusiasm a useful quality. Jacobitism, in short, was a romantic dream carried out by romantic dreamers.

The lukewarmness of the Scottish Jacobites, of which Colonel Hooke had complained so bitterly, was fatal to the success of the expedition of 1708, in many respects the best-timed and most skilfully organised of all the Jacobite expeditions. England was almost drained of her regular troops by the continental war, and

Scotland was practically undefended. Backed by 3000 or 4000 French regulars, the Jacobites might have scoured the country from end to end, apparently, without meeting with a moment's serious resistance. Yet when Admiral Fourbin with his little fleet reached Scotland, no response whatever was made to the preconcerted signals, and no encouragement whatever given to effect a landing. The Scottish Jacobites saw him come and saw him depart, knowing that he had with him the King, to whom they professed to be devoted, and 4000 regular troops to boot, and yet they made no sign.*

---

* Mr. Chambers, in his History of Scotland, puts it thus :—" In March, 1708, Fourbin arrived off the East coast with a considerable fleet, carrying 5000 men, and but *for some mismanagement* and the *accidental appearance* of the British Fleet, under Admiral Byng, he would have landed with these troops, and been *probably joined by an immense number of followers.*" From this statement we are led to imagine that the whole blame rested on Fourbin's shoulders, and that none was due to the backwardness of the Scottish Jacobites. A curious perversion of facts ! Equally curious is the statement that the appearance of the English fleet was "*accidental.*" Admiral Byng had for weeks been watching the port from which Fourbin sailed. The temporary dispersion of his ships by a storm enabled the Frenchmen to get to sea, but the English Admiral within a few hours was on his track, and chased him so closely right up the Frith of Forth that it was only by the superior sailing of

But there was a cause for this faint-heartedness among the Jacobites of Scotland. They had signally failed to gain over the Presbyterians to their side, and the Presbyterians were the backbone of the nation. Whatever success they may have had with individuals, they found all their attempts were vain to draw from the General Assembly of the Kirk a violent declaration against the Union. And it is impossible not to admire the dignity of the attitude assumed by the Scottish Kirk at this crisis. In the midst of all this passionate excitement and turbulent conflict, she stood true to her principles; no plausible promises, no artful temptations, no appeals to selfish interests, to national prejudices, to the memory of past wrongs, could lead her to forsake the first principles of her faith, and enter into unholy alliance with her sworn enemies, Prelacy and Popery. And the people were unquestion-

---

the French ships that they escaped, leaving one of their number in Byng's hands. But Jacobite writers will never admit that English vigilance had anything to do with the disconcertment of their plans.

ably influenced by the attitude of their Church. The fast appointed by the General Assembly to avert the impending invasion, and the uniform earnestness and solemnity with which it was observed, proved beyond doubt the true temper of the Presbyterians, and their unshaken loyalty to the theory of the Revolution. Even the Jacobites could not mistake or misrepresent such a significant expression of opinion, and reluctantly they abandoned all hope of co-operation from that quarter.

The action of the Presbyterians in 1708 should have taught the English Government the plain lesson that they had no worse enemies in Scotland than the Episcopalians, and no stauncher friends than the Presbyterians. Had they profited by that lesson they would have been spared much trouble and anxiety in the future. But with infatuated folly they refused to accept it, and allowed their prejudices against Nonconformists to overcome the dictates both of policy and justice. The Presbyterian Church was ill-rewarded for her faithful loyalty. When the fear of invasion had passed, she was wounded in her tenderest part by the Acts of Toleration and Abjuration, which cast a slur upon her loyalty and wantonly trampled upon those sensitive religious scruples which made the interference of the State in her devotional services seem nothing short of sacrilege and impiety. And then, as if she had not been already sufficiently hurt and humiliated, the hateful Act of Patronage was forced upon her, reviving a relic of Prelacy which she abhorred. All these measures were characterised not only by the grossest ingratitude and injustice, but by an insolent disregard for their religious sentiments and scruples, which was insufferably galling to the Presbyterians. And the same features marked all the policy of England towards Scotland at this period. English statesmen were at no pains to make themselves acquainted with either the character or the institutions of the Scottish people. The ignorance of the country and its laws displayed by the English Parliament was as extraordinary as it was disgraceful. With that arrogant assumption of superiority which is even yet a repulsive *trait* in the English character, the Government took it for granted that all existing Scottish institutions must be inferior to those in vogue in England, and that therefore the sooner they were supplanted by English institutions the better. On this principle, the collection of the taxes and revenue dues, a sufficiently odious and unpopular process in the best of hands, was not entrusted to Scotchmen or conducted on the Scotch system, but was handed over to English commissioners, who were even more ignorant of the customs of the country and the feelings of the inhabitants than their employers, and who rode roughshod over the national pride, and ran their heads at every turn against the national prejudices. The whole policy of England at this time was a tissue of offensive acts offensively done, many of them no doubt the result of ignorance, but ignorance

so gross and culpable as to bear all the appearance of deliberate insult. It is not wonderful
that under such circumstances Jacobite agitators
should have found little difficulty in persuading
the Scotch to believe that they were looked
upon as a subject people; indeed, the wonder
rather is that under such treatment the whole
nation did not rise as one man and indignantly
repudiate the Union.

It is needless to say that the Jacobites were
not idle at this time. It was an established
principle of their policy that everything which
tended to widen the breach between England
and Scotland was a clear gain to the Jacobite
cause. They hoped to win to their own party
all who were irritated by English policy, by
impressing upon them that the only chance of
obtaining a redress of grievances and a relief
from burdens lay in the repeal of the Union and
the restoration of the House of Stuart. Jacobitism now put on its brightest colours and most
engaging airs. All was concession and tolera-

tion. Papists, Prelatists, Presbyterians, were each and all to have everything they wanted, and exist together as a happy family; though secretly promises were made to each that it should be elevated at the expense of its rivals. It was not a time to be scrupulous about ways and means. The great thing to be achieved was to make the people unanimous in demanding a repeal of the Union. Let that be accomplished, and then it could be judged how far it was expedient to fulfil promises when the object for which they had been made was attained.

Such was the state of feeling in Scotland at the accession of George I., and if hostility towards England meant sympathy with Jacobitism, then never had the Jacobites been more powerful nor their prospects more hopeful.

The time had now come to test the real strength of Jacobitism in Scotland, by calling it into action. It was tried and found wanting, for it had no real hold on the hearts of the

E

people. There were a good many drouthy creatures who could drink bumpers of burgundy and stoups of usquebaugh without end to the health of King James and the success of his cause, but the exploits of these heroes began and ended over the bottle. They would drink for King Jamie with any man; but as to fighting for him, that was quite another matter, with which they had no concern. These pot-valiant Jacobites represented no inconsiderable section of the supporters of the House of Stuart, both in England* and Scotland, men who talked a great deal of blustering treason with a braggadocio

---

* Patten has the following sarcastic allusion to these pot-valiant Jacobites in his History of 1715:—"Indeed that party (the High Church,) who are never right hearty for the cause till they are mellow, as they call it, over a bottle or two, begin now to show us their blind side; and that is their just character, that they do not care for venturing their carcasses any farther than the tavern; there indeed, with their High Church and Ormond, they make one believe, who does not know them, that they would encounter the greatest opposition in the world; but after having consulted their pillows, and the fumes a little evaporated, it is to be observed of them that they generally become mighty tame, and are apt to look before they leap; and, with the snail, if you touch their houses, they hide their heads, shrink back and pull in their horns. I have heard Mr. Forster say he was blustered into this business by such people as these, but for the time to come he would never believe a drunken Tory."

air over their cups, but whose valour, like that of Bob Acres, oozed out at the palms of their hands when their heads were cool enough to appreciate danger. The utter worthlessness of such adherents was not discovered till the moment of action. Nor was the real spirit of the Presbyterians ascertained until subjected to the same test. Their bitterness against England they had been at no pains to conceal, and up to a certain point they had tolerated Jacobitism because there was this common bond of union between them. But when they saw Prelatists and Papists advocating a repeal of the Union more strongly than themselves, they felt there must be something wrong about a scheme which enlisted the sympathies of their deadliest enemies, and they at once relinquished their opposition and renounced all connexion with the Repeal movement. From the moment that the Presbyterians saw that by helping Jacobitism they would only be helping the cause of those religious sects whose views they detested and

abhorred, they never contemplated an alliance
with the Jacobites. They decided that it was
wisest to choose the lesser of two evils; and
there could be no question that Protestant
George of Hanover, with all his shortcomings,
and with the Union to boot, was better than
Popish James Stuart with his retinue of priests
and prelates.

I have said that Jacobitism had at this time
no real hold upon the hearts of the people of
Scotland. The rising of 1715 might seem to
refute that assertion. And indeed it has been
generally stated that the Jacobite party in 1715
comprised a majority, not only as to numbers,
but as to property in Scotland. There is really
no ground for that statement. Of the great
landed proprietors, Argyll, Queensberry, Montrose, Sutherland, Roxburgh, Hopetoun, Tweed-
dale, Annandale, Rothes, Marchmont, Stair,
Buchan, Lauderdale, Torphicen, Loudon, Had-
dington, were all of them at that time decided
Whigs, and favourable to the Hanoverian

succession ; and of the smaller proprietors south of the Forth, there were few who had not attached themselves to the same party. The Episcopalian gentry north of the Frith were, indeed, generally inclined to the Jacobite cause; but their tenants were not, and were only forced by violent compulsion to join the Jacobite army. The Lowland Scotch were universally opposed to the cause—they had had a little too much of the Stuarts, and wanted no more of them. The only real strength of the Jacobites lay in the Highlands, which included hardly an eighth of the population of Scotland. And even of the Highland clans, it is a mistake to suppose that all were Jacobites. There were many, such as the Campbells, the Sutherlands, the Mackays, the Rosses, the Monroes, the greater part of the Grants and Forbeses, and on this occasion the Frasers, who were on the side of the Government.

There are those who describe the rebellion of 1715 as the outburst of a long-pent-up national

spirit of Jacobitism. I have shown that this is
an utterly false view to take of it. The fact is,
that the rising of 1715 was not even really a
preconcerted measure. It was the rash act of a
single man, driven to desperation, smarting
under disgrace, conscious of detection, burning
for revenge. Let us glance for a moment at
the antecedents of the man on whose shoulders
rests all the responsibility of the rebellion of
1715.

John Erskine, Earl of Mar, had been the first
to bring the measure for the Union of the two
countries immediately before the Scottish Parliament. He had presented the draft of the
Act to appoint Commissioners to treat for the
Union. He had been himself made one of
those Commissioners, and had identified himself
with the Act of Union as one of its most enthusiastic supporters. As an acknowledgement
of his services, he had been made a Secretary
of State and Keeper of the Signet, with a special
pension attached. Add to this the fact that he

came of an old Protestant family, and it is clear
that every incident of his career had stamped
him as a staunch adherent of the Revolution
party, the very last man to cast in his lot with
the Jacobites. But to the very bottom of his
false heart Mar was a traitor and a knave.
And even at the English court his services,
though they had gained him rewards, had failed
to procure him respect. He was distrusted,
and he knew it. He knew also, on the death
of the Queen, that his enemies would use that
distrust to poison the mind of the new King
against him. He made a desperate effort,
therefore, to forestall them, and persuade the
Elector of his loyalty and devotion before en-
vious tongues had maligned him. While George
was yet in Hanover, Mar wrote to him in these
terms : " Your Majesty shall ever find me as
faithful and dutiful a subject and servant as ever
any of my family have been to the Crown, or as
I myself have been to my late mistress, the
Queen." In order to impress the King with

his power and influence in the Highlands, he
had also in his possession an address signed by
the principal chiefs in the Highlands, empower-
ing him to offer their entire allegiance to the
King. By what means he procured this document it is hard to say. But there can be no
doubt that without a thought of the chiefs whom
he was thus compromising, he would have
played this card to serve his own selfish ends.
He was not, however, able to present it, and he
therefore reserved it for another purpose, which
was fast ripening in his mind. In less than a
year from that time, a disgraced, chagrined, and
disappointed man, he was at the head of those
clans in armed revolt against the sovereign to
whom he had professed such ardent devotion.
And one of the means which he had used to
inflame their passions and their pride, was this
very protestation and offer of allegiance, which
he assured them had been scornfully flung back
in their teeth by the English king.

Like Montrose and Dundee, Mar found no

difficulty in raising the Highlanders in rebellion.
They had no stake in the peace or prosperity of
the kingdom, and were, as usual, ready to fight
on any side which could secure the allegiance of
their chiefs. That allegiance Mar had taken
measures to secure, and by a forged commission
from James induced the Jacobites to believe that
he was their King's accredited agent and viceroy
in Scotland.

In order to understand the success of this
sudden movement of Mar, it must be borne in
mind that a short time previously a great scheme
had been planned by the Jacobites at home and
abroad for a simultaneous invasion of England
and Scotland. Louis XIV. had promised the
assistance of a large force of French troops in
carrying out the scheme. The Duke of
Ormond was to lead the expedition against
England, and the Duke of Berwick that against
Scotland—and as they were both generals of
some capacity, the Jacobites were sanguine of
success. But there were two obstacles in the

way of an expedition leaving France, which the Jacobites had not taken into their calculations. The first was the English fleet, which was far more vigilant and active than its enemies have ever been willing to admit. The second, and by far the most formidable, was in the very heart of the French Court, in the person of John Dalrymple, Earl of Stair. The Whigs never did a shrewder stroke of policy than when they sent the Earl of Stair as ambassador extraordinary to the French Court. His vigilance was marvellous, his sources of information as infallible as they were mysterious. No plot, however carefully concealed, however warily planned, escaped his watchful eye. To the Jacobites the knowledge which he possessed of their most secret movements and machinations seemed nothing short of miraculous. He appeared to get wind of a conspiracy almost before the conspirators themselves had quite made up their minds that they were going to conspire. His system of *espionage* was perfect. The secret of it has never been thoroughly divulged, but we know that much of his information was procured by the treachery of ladies who were in the counsels of the Jacobite party. Among these, Mrs. Trant and Mdle. Chausseraye were afterwards notorious, though neither of them was at this time suspected by their own party. Stair himself was the model of a diplomatist; it is doubtful whether he has ever been equalled; it is certain that he has never been surpassed. Courteous, subtile, vigilant, resolute, too honest to be bribed, too courageous to be intimidated, too shrewd to be over-reached, it is impossible to overrate his influence upon French policy. So minute and accurate was his knowledge of every court intrigue, that the French Cabinet was literally over-awed; and his presence in Paris at this juncture did more to keep France neutral than all the fleets of Rooke, and all the *prestige* of Marlborough. He had full and early information of this great invasion scheme, and long before the expedition was ready to sail, the British

Government was in possession of complete details as to its design and destination. A vigorous and energetic remonstrance was at once forwarded to the French Government, who felt themselves compelled to disavow the expedition, which was consequently rendered abortive.

Now, Mar was perfectly aware of the failure of this scheme ; he knew, too, what excitement and preparation it had caused among the Scottish Jacobites. Before these effects had quite died away he resolved to strike a blow, for he knew not when so splendid an opportunity of avenging himself on the English Government might again present itself. His own personal influence in the Highlands was considerable; and, backed by a forged commission from James, he was confident that in the existing temper of the chiefs it would be irresistible. The result proved that he was right. The Jacobites had not yet wholly abandoned their attitude of expectancy—they were ready to act, and when Mar presented himself among them with his forged credentials,

and his announcement of the approach of the
promised succours from France, they took it for
granted that the original scheme had been re-
vived and was to be carried out in its entirety.
This delusion Mar fostered by the most unscrupulous and daring falsehoods, and the adherents of the Stuarts rallied eagerly round his
standard. And so, this one man, prompted
solely by mortified pride, and selfish disappointment, and personal resentment, plunged the
whole country into a civil war, and risked the
lives and properties of thousands in a cause for
which he had not one atom of affection, and
which he regarded only as an instrument to
further his own purposes.

The Pretender knew nothing of this insurrec-
tion until it was in full swing—it was too late
then to declare that it had been commenced
without his sanction ; and besides, as it promised
to be successful, his advisers thought it politic
to overlook Mar's deception, and condone the
forgery of the commission by issuing a fresh

one, which was secretly substituted for the forged document. Yet there can be little doubt that if the enterprize had not worn such a rosy hue at the commencement, they would have repudiated it altogether, and left Mar to bear all the odium of the failure. As it was, they not only countenanced it, but took to themselves the credit of having originated it, an assertion which none but Mar could contradict, and that only by criminating himself.

In a comparatively short time, Mar had collected the largest army that ever marched under the banner of the exiled Stuarts. But it had not been collected without difficulty. Recruits were only to be obtained in many cases by severe compulsion. The "Cross of Fire," indeed, had been sent through the Highlands after the gathering at Braemar, but it had lost its magic power, apathy had chilled the spirit of the Gael, the dread symbol no longer drew the plaided warriors from lonely mountain-side and sheltered glen in haste to the muster-place.

Other less romantic, but more efficacious, measures had to be resorted to on this occasion ; what
these were may be gathered from the following
letter of Mar to his bailiff at Kildrummie:
" Particularly, let my own tenants in Kildrummie
know, that if they come not forth with their best
arms, I will send a party immediately to burn
what they shall miss taking from them. And
they may believe this only a threat—but, by all
that's sacred, I'll put it in execution, let my loss
be what it will, that it may be an example to
others." Press-gangs from one clan were employed to kidnap recruits from another, and thus
the ranks of the Jacobite army were filled. The
prisoners taken afterwards at Preston declared
at their trial that they had been driven like
cattle to take arms, and that they had no option
whatever in the matter. In fact, they served as
little by choice as French conscripts or British
pressed-sailors. It was the same in 1745.
Marchant says, "At Dundee, the Duke of
Perth killed two of his own farmers for refusing

to rise at his command; and the Lord Ogilvie was very cruel to every one who denied him for the same reason." These are specimens of the gentle persuasion required to induce the loyal Jacobites of the Highlands to take arms for their beloved Sovereign! After this, who can say that even in the Highlands Jacobitism had any hold on the affections of the people? Under such circumstances there is little cause for wonder in the fact that Mar succeeded in collecting a large army, and still less cause for wonder that his soldiers should have deserted by hundreds whenever they had a chance.

It is only justice to Mar to admit that though he was solely responsible for the rising of 1715, he was quite aware of his own incapacity as a leader, and would have gladly given up the command to any one who would have taken it off his hands. But, strange to say, no one coveted the distinction of commanding the Jacobite army. The Duke of Atholl refused the proffered honour point-blank; the Earl of Seaforth delayed his arrival to avoid it; the Marquis of Huntley allowed his religion to be pleaded as a bar without a murmur, and indeed, probably himself suggested the disqualification. And so, Mar was forced to take the command of the movement, which his own selfishness, and reck-lessness, and petulance, had called into being. We have no record of his personal feelings, but it is hardly too much to imagine that they were akin to those with which the hero of Mrs. Shelley's wild romance viewed the monster which his own hands had created.

And meanwhile, what were the temper and attitude of the great bulk of the Scottish people? They were essentially loyal to the House of Hanover. In the presence of immediate danger, they remembered that freedom, and security, and toleration, were blessings not likely to result from a restoration of the Stuarts. The spirit which animated them showed itself in the Appeal of the Edinburgh Association, where almost for the first time in the history of the period we

F

find the benefits of the Revolution calmly and sensibly recognised. A short extract will serve to illustrate its character :—" Can we without horror remember the unparalleled cruelties we met with when a Popish interest and faction had the ascendant ? Can we forget the remarkable deliverance God made for us in breaking the yoke of the arbitrary and tyrannical government, by the great King William, in the late glorious Revolution ?" And much more in the same strain, showing that Scotchmen did at last appreciate the blessings of the Revolution. The effect of the appeal was instantaneous. In every town there sprung up a body of loyal men ready to take arms for the House of Hanover. Edinburgh had her Associated Volunteers, Glasgow her Burgher Guard, Dumfries its Company of Loyal Bachelors, and Greenock and Paisley were not behind hand in contributing their quota of citizen soldiers. There was not a single town or burgh of any size that did not give such practical proofs of its loyalty as these. Had

England taken advantage of this burst of enthusiasm, and given it timely encouragement, I believe Scotland would alone and unaided have crushed out the rebellion. But such a policy did not commend itself to the wisdom of English statesmen. The ministry, still ridiculously prejudiced against Nonconformism in every shape and form, looked with cold disfavour upon this ebullition of Presbyterian loyalty. They feared that it would clash with other interests, and his Majesty was therefore advised to answer the loyal address of the Edinburgh Association with an intimation that *sufficient measures had already been adopted to secure the defence of the country, and that he wished to save his loyal subjects further trouble and expense!* Now, as it was notorious that there were not at that moment three complete regiments of regular troops in Scotland, and that England herself was not in a position to scrape together a regular army half the size of Mar's, the absurdity of this statement was patent to every Scotchman, and the insult which it conveyed was seen and felt at once. As might have been expected, a sensitive and high-spirited nation was indignant and disgusted at conduct so cold, so unsympathetic, so ungrateful—and there was never again the same readiness displayed to make sacrifices or take arms for the House of Hanover.

It is not necessary to dwell upon the military features of the affair of 1715. The mere fact that Argyll, with a force of scarcely 3000 men, was able to hold his own against an army of upwards of 16,000 men, is sufficient proof of the incapacity of the Jacobite leaders. But even their incapacity could hardly have deprived them of complete success had the forces under Macintosh and Forster advanced to join Mar instead of pursuing their mad and infatuated march into England. Argyll, thus caught between two fires, must have been crushed, and all Scotland would have been at their feet. What the result would have been in that case is of course only matter for vague conjecture; but such a success might have procured them the assistance of France, so long promised, so long withheld, and the whole current of events might have been changed. But "the Gods willed otherwise."

It was in the full expectation of finding the whole of Scotland in the hands of his victorious generals that James, deceived by the glowing rhapsodies of Mar, landed in his kingdom shortly after the fatal disasters of Preston and Sherriff-muir. His first sight of the shattered remnants of Mar's dispirited and retreating army dashed those hopes to the ground. It was a cruel and unexpected blow, and James succumbed to it at once. He showed too plainly by his looks that he despaired of his cause ; and his presence, instead of raising, most effectually damped the spirits of his followers.

At no time was his personal appearance prepossessing. The thin frame, enfeebled by dissipation—the languid air—the dull sodden eye— were not the characteristics of a hero. James did not possess a single quality calculated to win the hearts of his Scottish subjects. He was a bigot and a coward. He had no sympathy with his British lieges, and he showed that he had none. If George I. was a German, James was a Frenchman in heart and soul, and the one was not more a foreigner in spirit than the other. As licentious as Charles the Second,* the Pretender had none of the Merry Monarch's *bon-hommie.* His profligacy was dull and stupid. It had not even that false and meretricious attractiveness which vice sometimes has when allied to a genial temperament. It required no very deep student of physiognomy to perceive that this stolid and sensual face was not the face of a generous Prince. And yet this was the

---

* "The heir of one of the greatest names, of the greatest kingdoms, and of the greatest misfortunes in Europe, was often content to lay the dignity of his birth and grief at the wooden shoes of a French chambermaid, and to repent afterwards (for he was very devout), in ashes taken from the dust pan. 'Tis for mortals such as these that nations suffer, that parties struggle, that warriors fight and bleed ! A year afterwards gallant heads were falling, and Nithisdale in escape, and Derwentwater on the scaffold ; whilst the heedless ingrate for whom they risked and lost all was tippling with his seraglio of mistresses in his *petite maison* of Chaillot."—*Thackeray, Esmond.*

man of whom Mar had told his Highland followers—"Without any compliment to him, and to do him nothing but justice, set aside his being a prince, he is really the finest gentleman I ever saw." Lying was constitutional with the Earl, he gave way to it on the slightest occasion, and so he proceeded to dilate on "the good presence," the "fine parts," the affability and sweet temper of this paragon of princes, whom he declared "to be too good for his subjects; to have him, is more than they deserve!" Even this piece of flattery, however, was outdone by the Episcopal clergy of Aberdeen, who presented an address to the Pretender on his arrival in their city, in which they had the effrontery to utter this astounding falsehood:—"Your princely virtues are such that, in the opinion of the best judges, you are worthy to wear a crown though you had not been born to it!" Could the force of flunkeyism go further? The bluff Highlanders, who were at least honest in the expression of their opinion, made no attempt to conceal

their disappointment and disgust at the unkingly
appearance of their King. They set great store
on physical gifts. They expected a man—they
found an automaton.*

Had the Duke of Argyll pressed the Jacobites with any degree of vigour after the battle of
Sheriff-Muir, there can be little doubt that the
Pretender would have fallen into his hands, and
the Rebellion would have been summarily stamped out instead of being allowed to die a lingering
death. And such a stern suppression would
probably have rendered the rising of '45 impossible. But Argyll was a thoroughly fickle and
selfish politican; he could not make up his mind
to devote himself honestly to any one side or
party. He thought that Jacobitism might, perhaps, have sufficient vitality left in it yet to make
it worth his while to keep on good terms with
its supporters. His dilatory and vacillating

---

* The Highlanders, struck with James's cadaverous looks and want of
animation, asked repeatedly whether he was not an automaton. — See
" *Account by a Rebel Officer at Perth.*"

movements, therefore, were prompted by treasonable motives. And of this the Government
was so well aware, that when the Rebellion was
at an end they showed how little they attributed
the result to any conduct of his, by disgracing
him, and depriving him of his appointments—a
punishment which he richly merited.

So ended, with the ignominious flight of James
and Mar, the Jacobite Rebellion of 1715, an
enterprize as feebly executed as it was rashly
conceived.

The conduct of the Government after the
suppression of the Rebellion has met with much
severe censure on the ground of its cruelty. I
think the charge is both unjust and undeserved.
Not more than thirty persons in all, including
the Earl of Derwentwater and Lord Kenmure,
were executed. That there was not much real
vindictiveness against the rebels may be gathered
from the general feeling of relief which per-
vaded the country at the news of the Earl of
Nithisdale's escape, a feat which he would

probably never have accomplished without the connivance of his gaolers. The King himself could not conceal his satisfaction when the announcement was made to him, but exclaimed heartily that "It was the best thing a man in his condition could have done." The number of escapes from prison was too great to have been the effect of accident. It was generally felt that it would not be politic to shed too much blood—and yet to pardon all the offenders would only give encouragement to rebellions in the future. The conduct of the Government, so far from being vindictive and bloodthirsty, displayed as much mercy and moderation as was consistent with the safety of established institutions and the vindication of the rights of the people.

The alarm and excitement of the Rebellion were succeeded in Scotland by a calm, during which Church matters chiefly occupied public attention. In this season of tranquillity the prosperity of the country advanced with gigantic strides. Yet, underlying all this appearance of contentment, there was a current of discontent, daily acquiring fresh strength from new griev- ances, which were the offspring of a condition of peace and wealth. The great Lowland land- owners had found it more profitable to convert their estates into immense pastures for cattle than to allow them to remain split up into small arable farms. To effect this change they had to eject a large number of small farmers, to make room for their enormous herds; and the ejected farmers in consequence suffered great distress, which in many cases, there is reason to believe, was purposely aggravated by Jacobite landown- ers, in order to goad the farmers into fury and raise a spirit of discontent favourable to the promotion of Jacobite schemes. Riots ensued; and though they were easily suppressed, they left a sore feeling in the country, which accounted for the apathy with which the Lowland peasantry and gentry, in 1745, regarded the progress of the Jacobite arms and the danger which threat- ened the institutions to which they had heretofore been loyal. Then there was the Malt-Tax agitation in the large towns—the resolute and systematic resistance to the payment of revenue dues, which turned the whole nation, with the honourable exception of Glasgow, into a smuggling community—and, arising out of this, the famous Porteous riots, which stirred the passions of the people, and roused a good deal of the old animosity against England. All these things were so many helps to Jacobitism, and the Jacobites judiciously availed themselves of them.

But meanwhile there had been growing up in the country a spurious form of Jacobitism, which, as distinguished from political and practical, I may call sentimental or romantic Jacobitism. In later years it wholly supplanted the other, and was professed by those whose political principles were utterly opposed to the doctrines of genuine Jacobitism. As I shall have to deal with the subject more in detail, when considering the ballad-literature of Jacobitism, I will only say here that it owed its origin to those satirical

and pathetic ballads, and was founded on a
sentiment of pity.   Pity of itself, however, is not
a sufficiently powerful form of sympathy to
induce men to launch out into active measures;
and the Jacobites, who had built great hopes
upon the wide-spread diffusion of this sentimental Jacobitism, found this to their cost—found
that they had mistaken a shallow sentiment for
a settled creed.   I attribute both the success
and the failure of the Rebellion of 1745 to the
existence of this sentimental Jacobitism, and the
false hopes which it excited.   Without the
enthusiasm which it inspired among those whose
sympathies and principles were already Jacobite,
that expedition would never have been possible;
but at the same time the deceptive promise of
deeper loyalty and devotion which it gave, lured
the Jacobites to their ruin.   It is a remarkable
and significant fact, that with all the enthusiasm
which his appearance excited, Charles Edward
was never at any time able to gather under his
standard even half the number of men that had

followed Mar in 1715. No better proof than
this is needed to show that Scottish Jacobitism
was a sentiment and not a principle.

In making this assertion I do not forget that
there were some families, both in Scotland and
England, in which the " Jacobite tradition " was
an abiding principle, which neither lapse of time
nor change of circumstances could destroy; it
was a strange fanatical enthusiasm, not amenable to reason, not to be defended by logic, but
so strong and so earnest that those who held it
would, without a moment's hesitation, under any
circumstances, and at any time, have given up
life and lands—home, and health, and liberty,
for the sake of the House of Stuart.

As to the real feelings of the great bulk of
shrewd and sensible Scotchmen, I have seen
them nowhere more soberly and clearly set forth
than in a letter written in 1745 (at the very time
when Charles Edward was blockading Edinburgh
Castle, and issuing manifestos from Holyrood),
by Mr. Craik, a Dumfriesshire laird, to the

young Earl of Nithisdale, from which I quote
the following extract:—"The present family,"
he says, "have now reigned over us these thirty
years; and though during so long a time they
may have fallen into errors, or may have committed faults (as what Government is without?),
yet I will defy the most sanguine zealot to find
in history a period equal to this in which Scotland possessed so uninterrupted a felicity—in
which liberty, civil and religious, was so universally enjoyed by all people, of whatever denom-
ination—nay, by the open and avowed enemies
of the family and constitution—or a period in
which all ranks of men have been so effectually
secured in their property. Have not trade,
manufactures, agriculture, and the spirit of industry in our own country extended themselves
further during this period, and under this family,
than for ages before? Has any man suffered
in his liberty, life, or fortune, contrary to law?
Stand forth and name him if you can. Though
the King's person, his family, his government,

and his ministers have been openly abused a thousand times in the most scurrilous and reproachful terms, could it ever provoke him to one arbitrary act, or to violate those laws which he had made the rule of his government? Look into the reigns of the Jameses and the Charleses, and tell me whether these divine and hereditary princes were guided by the same spirit of mildness and forgiveness." There we have fairly represented not only the sentiments of Scotchmen, but also the actual condition of Scotland.

But while the Lowlands had thus increased in wealth and prosperity, the Highlands had remained stagnant—the inhabitants were at least a century behind their neighbours in civilization—they had no idea of utilizing their natural resources and advantages, but were dependent upon fishing and the humblest forms of agriculture for subsistence. Hence the abject poverty of the Highlanders; which was not confined to the lower classes, but extended even to the greatest nobles. To such shifts were they driven

to obtain money, that one nobleman, whose
name was a tower of strength in the Highlands,
derived by far the larger portion of his revenues
from a gambling-house which he had the privilege
·of keeping in London, whilst another owned and
occasionally served in a glover's shop in Ayr.
So that there is no lack of precedents for modern
Scottish noblemen desirous of sending their
sons "into business." It is hard for us now to
conceive the absolute poverty of these great
Highland Chiefs—many of whom scarcely knew
what it was to possess as much as ten shillings
at one time. It was this poverty, pervading all
classes, which made the Highlanders, from the
chief to the gillie, hail any new adventure with
delight as a possible means of repairing their
desperate fortunes. And this practical consideration won more recruits for the Stuarts than any
sentiments of chivalry or romance. At the same
time it is only just to add, that it enhances
tenfold the fidelity, and devotion, and chivalrous
honour of the Highlanders towards their fugitive

Prince with £30,000 upon his head, to remember how great and strong were the temptations both to high and low to betray him. The reward of treachery would have enriched a whole clan for ever. And though fear was, perhaps, the strongest element in a Highlander's fidelity, yet, giving both to fear and superstition their full due, there is a residuum of nobleness and high-minded generous feeling left, which it is impossible not to admire; and that heart must be callous indeed which does not feel some thrill of sympathetic pride in a quality which so signally adorns and elevates our common human nature. I do not believe in the innate loyalty to the House of Stuart which enthusiastic and fanatical Jacobites claim as a feature of the Highland clans, I think it never had any existence but in the imaginations of writers who knew very little of the real temper and habits of the Highlanders; but I do believe in the simple, sincere, and single-hearted spirit of chivalry and honour which kept them faithful to a fallen prince and a ruined cause, and which has given the Jacobite Episode of 1745 a romantic interest that Time will never lessen nor critical investigation destroy.

It would be superfluous to dwell upon the events of 1745, seeing that they have been celebrated by the pens both of historians and romancers, though I confess it is often difficult to decide where history ends and romance begins, for the two have generally gone hand in hand. In looking at the results of 1745, however, it must be remembered that though far more prolific in events than the rebellion of 1715, it was not full of such deep significance and importance to the Constitution. The rebellion of 1715 was the test and trial of the Hanoverian succession; the Stuart dynasty ended in Anne; it was to be seen whether the country would really accept a King who was a foreigner, and whether Whig principles would stand the strain upon them. There was no such significance or importance about the affair of

1745. The temper of the people had already been tried, and proved to be, if not hostile to Jacobitism, at least wholly indifferent to it. No one who knew the forces at the disposal of the English Government—the moral force which lay in the passive contentment of the people with their existing institutions—the physical force which lay in vastly superior armies—ever thought for a moment that the success of the Jacobite raid was within the range of possibility. Lazy indifference or idle curiosity represented the general attitude of the great mass of the people in England,* and there was a disposition to let the matter go on unchecked for a while to see what would come of it, so confident was the Government of being able to crush the rebellion whenever it chose to exert itself. The throne of England was never for one moment in danger, and had not the Jacobite leaders wisely resolved on a retreat when they reached Derby, there can be little doubt that not a single man of

---

* See Letter from Gray to Walpole in the latter's published correspondence,

their army would ever have left England alive. This was the opinion and belief of the Jacobite chiefs themselves, with the sole exception of Charles himself, who, with the foolish infatuation and hot-headed impetuosity of a school-boy, urged an advance upon London. The Chevalier de Johnstone, who was with the Jacobite army as aide-de-camp, both to the Prince and Lord George Murray, and whose opinions on military matters are always entitled to weight, says plainly, "If we had continued to advance to London, and had encountered all the troops of England, with the Hessians and Swiss in its pay, there was every appearance of our being immediately exterminated, without the chance of a single man escaping. Bravery, even when carried the length of ferocity, cannot effect impossibilities, and must necessarily yield to numbers."

There is a further contrast between 1715 and 1745 in this circumstance, that, while in the former the tardy appearance of the Pretender was distinctly detrimental to the cause, in the latter the presence of the Prince was the chief reason for the temporary success of the movement. For there can be no doubt that nine-tenths of the enthusiasm which greeted Charles Edward was a tribute paid to his personal attractions, and not to the cause which he represented. Canny burghers and tender-hearted dames wished "God-speed" to the young Prince, whose "bonny" face and gracious manners took their sympathies by storm, though beyond good-wishes they were too prudent and cautious to venture. And, indeed, Charles had every physical gift of a popular leader. Handsome, amiable, high-spirited, of striking appearance, and singularly fascinating manners, he had also the address to turn these natural endowments to the very best advantage. He laid himself out to captivate every one, and he succeeded. He flattered the vanity, he appealed to the pride, of Scotchmen of all classes. And, enchanted by such condescension from a Prince, the thought never occurred to them that this was all a piece of clever acting—a necessary adjunct to the *rôle* which he had undertaken, and the character which he had assumed. His success was naturally greatest among the women, he danced with them, he smiled upon them—and forthwith they were devoted Jacobites. And historians have quite overlooked, I think, the importance of their influence upon his fortunes. It is difficult to overrate the power which the women of a country possess when they are animated, as in this case, by one strong and common sentiment. An eloquent but paradoxical modern writer has stated his opinion that all war is woman's fault; that at any moment she might put an end to it with less trouble than she takes every day to go out to dinner, and that if every lady in the upper classes of civilized Europe would simply vow that while any cruel war proceeds she will wear *black*, a mute's black—with no jewel, no ornament, no excuse for or evasion into prettiness— no war would last a week.* And looking at the

* Ruskin.—" Crown of Wild Olive."

results of women's influence recorded in history, I do not think there is nearly as much extravagance and exaggeration in that statement as in most of Mr. Ruskin's utterances. Be this as it may, there can be no doubt that feminine influence had a very powerful effect in paving the way for Charles Edward's success in Scotland. Lord-Advocate Forbes recognised that influence, and complains bitterly of it. Speaking of 1745, he says, in one of his letters, "All Jacobites, how prudent soever, became mad; all doubtful people became Jacobites; and all bankrupts became heroes, and talked of nothing but hereditary right and victory; and, what was more grievous to men of gallantry, and if you will believe me, *much more mischievous to the country*, all the fine ladies, if you will except one or two, became passionately fond of the young Adventurer, and used all their arts and industry for him in the most intemperate manner." What Charles Edward afterwards owed to the heroism and devotion of a woman every child knows, and yet this man, who was more indebted to women than any other man living, perhaps, could write thus of them in his later years—" As for men, I have studied them closely, and were I to live till fourscore I could scarcely know them better than I do; but as for women, I have thought it useless, they being so much more wicked and impenetrable"! Such was the gratitude of a Stuart!

Of the personal character of Charles Edward, putting aside these outward graces and attractions, there is not much to be said that is favourable. But it would be unfair to pass any judgment upon his character, without taking into consideration the surroundings amidst which he had been brought up. The moral atmosphere of that mock-court at Rome would have been fatal to the growth of any young life. Meddlers of all kinds, ruined soldiers, broken-down statesmen, shifty priests, surrounded the two boys then growing up to an inheritance of false hopes and idle greatness.* There they were taught to cherish absurd and extravagant notions of the royal prerogative and the divine right of kings. And the result was, that Charles Edward never felt that gratitude for the services rendered him by his followers in Scotland which they expected and deserved, because it never occurred to him that they were doing anything more than their duty. He accepted the sacrifices made in his behalf as his right, and he could not see that any particular credit attached to acts which were in his view the simple duties which a subject owed to his sovereign. Hence the charge of ingratitude against him. But it would be a thankless task to dwell upon all his faults. Superficially he was a high-spirited and amiable young man—impetuous and sanguine, but with not one of the solid qualities of a leader or a ruler. He was essentially a weak man, a creature of impulse. Not a single exploit in the Jacobite Episode of

* See a graphic description in Mrs. Oliphant's "Historical Sketches of the Reign of George II.," from which these details are taken.

1745 can be traced to any skill or daring of his—
or to any spark of military dash, invention, or
genius on his part. Whenever he interfered he
did mischief. It was he who proposed, and,
against the advice of all his wisest counsellors,
insisted upon the march into England. Whenever his wilful obstinacy was opposed, he knew
that he had but to cast a taunt of cowardice in
the teeth of the oldest Highland chief to scatter
all his prudence and judgment to the winds,
and he meanly and ungenerously availed himself of this weapon whenever the wiser counsels
of his veterans clashed with his own impetuous
schemes. When he was unable to carry his
wild project of advancing upon London from
Derby, he behaved like a spoiled child deprived
of a toy. He was by turns reckless, sullen, and
passionate. From that time he displayed no
manliness, no fortitude, nor any single great or
good quality. His character could not stand the
searching test of adversity, and, unfortunately,
he had a more than ordinary share of that bitter

medicine. Without accepting any of the extreme charges against him, and leaving out of sight his miserable end, I cannot see how any candid critic of his character can for a moment endorse the eulogies of those who maintain that he was the best of all the Stuarts, and that, had he come to the throne, his virtues as a monarch would have transcended those of any of his predecessors. These are the foolish exaggerations of prejudiced and fanatical partizans, and I see nothing in the character of Charles Edward, as fairly portrayed by the hands of unbiassed limners, to lead me to regret for one moment that he never ascended the throne of Great Britain.

The young Prince having been the life and soul of the enterprize of 1745, it naturally collapsed as soon as he withdrew from it. But there were many who believed that Culloden was far from a decisive battle, and that had the Prince presented himself at the gathering of Highlanders, which took place shortly afterwards at Ruthven, he might have continued the struggle with no small chance of success. It is certain that the Highlanders were terribly disappointed at his declining to listen to their earnest entreaty to come and put himself at their head, and, with sullen reluctance, dispersed to their homes, vowing that for the second time they had been abandoned by a Prince at the crisis when his presence was most needed. Of the cruelties which stained the victory of Culloden, so much has been said that it would be idle to say more. Leaving a wide margin for exaggeration, they were still inexcusable, though probably not worse than those which usually mark the suppression of a rebellion—very little, if any, worse for example than those inflicted upon the Sepoys after the Mutiny of 1859. The Duke of Cumberland was indeed a strict martinet, and had been brought up in a stern school, but he was not the ferocious fiend which his enemies have repre-sented him. His heart was not impervious to generous and tender sentiments, though he

certainly had few of these to spare for the rebels.
But then there was a cause for this sternness.
He knew that it was the intention of the rebel
generals, had they been victorious, to show no
quarter to the English troops, for Lord George
Murray's orders for the day fell into his hands,
and they were as follows:—

"It is His Royal Highness's positive orders
that every person attach himself to some corps
of the army, and remain with the corps night
and day until the battle and pursuit be finally
over, and *to give no quarter to the Elector's troops
on no account whatsoever.* This regards the foot
as well as the horse. The order of battle is to
be given to every general officer, and every
commander of a regiment or squadron. It is
required and expected of each individual in the
army, as well officer as soldier, that he keep the
post he shall be allotted; and if any man turn
his back to run away, the next behind such man
is to shoot him. Nobody, upon pain of death, to
strip the slain or plunder until the battle is over.

The Highlanders to be kilts, and nobody to throw away their guns.

(Signed), GEORGE MURRAY,

Lieutenant-General."

There has never been any satisfactory explanation of this order from the Jacobite point of view, nor have there been any proofs adduced to support the assertion that it was a forgery. And the marked difference in the conduct of the Royal troops before and after Culloden, is favourable to the theory that the exasperation caused by this revelation of the intentions of the rebels prompted many of the excesses perpetrated by the English soldiery after their victory. It is not the only instance of Jacobite cruelty to be met with in the annals of Jacobitism. The devastation of Auchterarder in 1715, the abandonment of the garrison of Carlisle in 1745, the deliberate proposal of a Scottish gentleman of high rank to cut off the thumbs of all the prisoners taken at Falkirk, in order to incapacitate them from holding muskets, are not very creditable to the humanity of those concerned in them.

In considering the ruthless measures adopted by the Duke of Cumberland in stamping out the Rebellion, it must, however, be remembered that to him the Jacobites were merely rebels taken in arms against their lawful sovereign. In his eyes they were not invested with any of that romantic heroism with which a later age has credited them. They were just commonplace insurrectionists, and nothing more; and it is unreasonable to expect that a victorious general, who has just overcome a determined resistance, should regard his enemies with that generous appreciation which is only possible to the dispassionate critics of a subsequent generation. And it must also be remembered that it is peculiarly characteristic of the Jacobite insurrections, and the incidents connected with them, that they have been viewed through the coloured light of feelings arising since their extinction, instead of in that cold light of truth which at the time surrounded the deeds done and the men who did them.

The judicial executions which supplemented Cumberland's rigorous measures have also been subjected to the harshest criticism, which is not wholly undeserved. But the arguments adduced in favour of greater clemency are certainly not such as to convince us that the English Government was transgressing the bounds of reasonable severity. Take the following as an example:— " Men so true to an ill-fated cause would have been faithful to any engagements which required them to abandon their efforts in that cause, under the influence of gratitude for clemency, but too imperfectly understood in those turbulent and merciless times." * The sophistry of that argument is patent. If really faithful to the cause, such men would have died rather than have disowned it. If they had renounced it, would not the fact that they had been faithless to one cause

* Thomson's " Memoirs of the Jacobites."

under pressure of circumstances, render their fidelity to another suspicious? But men like these would have given no pledge to bind them to abandon the cause which they had served so devotedly, would it then have been wise or safe to set them free without any guarantee of their abstaining from all insurrectionary movements in the future?* The experience of 1715 gave a direct answer in the negative.

But it is not on the inglorious triumph of Culloden, nor on its dark and bloodstained sequel, that our thoughts dwell in contemplating the episode of 1745. It is rather on that gallant

---

* "No government can extend to defeated insurgents the privilege of prisoners of war, without opening the way to continued insecurity and causing more public misery than the utmost severity can create. The security which nations have against the turbulent dispositions of their neighbours is, that they cannot be assailed by isolated collections of individuals; the State itself must make war. But if a government were to treat all the individual subjects who disturb its order with the etiquette due to nations making war with it, all guarantee for internal tranquillity would vanish. No diplomatic interchanges, no consultations of other powers, no formal government arrangements and preliminaries would be necessary. Whenever interest or passion excited them with sufficient force, bands of the people would rise against any government, however beneficent, if the alternative were success or a treaty without punishment."—*Burton*, Vol. II., pp. 207-8.

"The rebel who bravely ventures has forfeited his life."—*Gibbon*.

young hero who forms its central figure—on his brief and meteoric course—the short fourteen months of glory in which his sun shone so brightly, only to be wrapped in clouds before its noon, and to set in darkness and disgrace. Nor do I envy the man whose heart denies all sympathy to the outlawed Prince—wandering, hunted, and forlorn, through the wild western islands—or whose imagination cannot realize the mournful pathos of the exile's last farewell, as with tearful eyes and bursting heart he takes his last look at the land of his hopes—the scene of his dazzling and romantic triumph—while the little vessel bears him away from it for ever, to close a bright career in the pursuit of sordid ends and the indulgence of ignoble vices.

It has been my object in the present essay rather to trace the feelings and sentiments of the Scottish people, and show their bearing upon political events, than to give any connected narrative of historical incidents. And I should, therefore, be omitting a very important feature, were I to conclude without some remarks on the literature of the period, where it is but natural to look for the best reflex of the national sentiments. I shall confine myself to the literature which illustrates those sentiments, and pass over the purely historical chronicles which the period produced.

And, first, there are the personal records of those who were actors in these events, to whom we are indebted for an insight into the characters of the prominent men of the time, and the motives which prompted their actions. Of these, the limited space at my disposal will only allow me to touch upon a few of the most important. Taking them in order of time, I notice first the *Memoirs of Lochiel*. These Memoirs, supposed to have been written by Sir John Drummond, supply much interesting and valuable information as to the early period of the Jacobite episode. They are the history of an epoch as well as the record of the career of

a great man. For Ewen Cameron, the subject
of them, was that famous Lochiel of whom
General Monk wrote in his despatches, "No
oath shall be required of Lochiel to Cromwell,
but his word to live in peace"; he was Dundee's
right hand in 1689, and he survived to witness
the rising of 1715. These memoirs of his life
and times, therefore, embrace the whole of the
first portion of the Jacobite episode; and they
are remarkable not only for the light they throw
upon the career of a chieftain who, take him for
all in all, had no equal either in ability or influence among all his Scottish contemporaries,
but also as giving sketches of the characters of
most of the leading men in Scotland at that
time, sketches drawn from personal observation,
and, though necessarily biassed, yet on the
whole commendably moderate in tone.

Very different are the *Lockhart Papers*, by
George Lockhart, of Carnwath, a most pronounced, and I might almost say, fierce Jacobite,
the character of which may be surmised from the

fact that it was their author's intention that they should not be published until after his death, when public feeling should have calmed down, and when the disclosures which they contained could hurt no one. But the manuscript was lent to a faithless friend, who gave it to a public scrivener to transcribe, and the latter kept back a copy which he sold to a publisher. They were published in 1719, and, to Lockhart's dismay, this outspoken expression of opinion, with all its bitter criticisms and severe strictures, burst like a thunderbolt upon friends and foes alike, and created consternation and commotion everywhere. The style of the Papers is caustic and incisive, full of happy and often brilliant touches of satire and irony. They are marked, too, by a fair and candid tone, except when the authors of the Union come under the writer's scalpel. Then his wrath and indignation are too much for his judgment. Indeed, he confesses as much. "'Tis true," he says, "my indignation against the betrayers of my country is so great

I never could nor will speak or write otherwise of them; but, when it does not induce me to deviate from the truth, on so provoking a subject I may be granted that grain of allowance which you know is never refused losing gamesters." That allowance I am sure all readers, whatever their political opinions, will be ready to grant in consideration of the amusement and information which the Papers afford them.

The *Memoirs of the Master of Sinclair* cover the same period, and are of a somewhat similar type, but with the bitterness and satire intensified tenfold. To such extreme lengths does the author carry his acrid sarcasm, that Sir Walter Scott, although he supplied an Introduction and Notes to the Memoirs, was deterred from publishing them lest the malignant and scathing criticism of contemporaries should even then give pain to persons still living, and the Memoirs consequently remained unpublished till 1858. They abound in graphic and sarcastic pictures of the depravity, meanness, profligacy, and treachery, which were the most prominent characteristics of the times. The Master of Sinclair had been chief of " The Grumblers," as they were called, in Mar's camp, and upon Mar he pours all the vials of his wrath and bitterness. Indeed, the persistent malignity of his attack defeats its object, and there was surely no need to devote so much energy and earnestness to the task of painting Mar in blacker colours than those in which he appeared to all who knew him. Like Lockhart, the Master rages with impotent fury against the Treaty of Union—he calls it Mar's first and greatest political crime, " the blackest and atrociousest of crimes, never to be forgiven by God Almighty, and I think ought never to be forgiven and impossible to be forgotten by men." It is a characteristic of these Memoirs, and indeed of all the contemporary records of personal experience and opinion, that they contain a complete exposure of the motives and conduct of the men who figured in the

Jacobite intrigues, and by introducing us to the actors, and enabling us to hear what they have to say of one another, utterly disperse those notions of the singleness of purpose, the disinterested devotion, and the untarnished honour of the Jacobite leaders which romancers have striven to inculcate. From the revelations here given we find that the chief object of a public man of those days was to find out which side it would best suit his own ends to belong to for the time being, and that he would go to extreme shifts of meanness and treachery to assure himself on this important point. The ordinary vision of a Jacobite hero, chivalrous and self-sacrificing, vanishes into thin air when we are thus let behind the scenes. But what the Master of Sinclair tells us of his contemporaries must be taken *cum grano salis*, for his own antecedents will not bear close investigation. His two so-called duels with the brothers Schaw were murders, pure and simple, and there is plenty of contemporary evidence to show that he was ruthless, vindictive, ferocious, and malignant. His sketches of his fellow-rebels are trenchant and clever; but when he describes them as a collection of knaves and cut-throats, worse than the riff-raff that followed David to the Cave of Adullam, one is inclined to say, that, if it were so, they could hardly have had a fitter companion than the Master himself, whose portrait I think is pretty correctly hit off in the following stanza of a contemporaneous ballad:—

> The master with the bully's face,
>   And with the coward's heart,
> Who never failed, to his disgrace,
>   To act a coward's part.

The *Culloden Papers* are another important contribution to the literature which really reflects the manners and sentiments of the period. They are a collection of documents selected and arranged from papers discovered in Culloden House, the family mansion of the Forbeses, in 1812, and consist chiefly of correspondence ranging over the period from 1625–1748. The later portion, containing the correspondence of Duncan Forbes, Lord Advocate, is the most interesting, enriched as it is by letters from Sir Robert Walpole, the Dukes of Newcastle and Argyll, Lords Hardwicke and Mansfield, Speaker Onslowe, General Oglethorpe, and many others in England, besides all the famous men in Scotland without exception. Not the least valuable item in their contents are the Memoranda of Duncan Forbes himself, representing a view taken on the spot of a period of Scottish history and manners the features of which are well worthy to be retained, although the last links which bound it to our own age are now dissolved. But here, as in the Memoirs already referred to, the most important feature is the clue which these letters afford to the motives which prompted the Highland chiefs to join the Pretender. So far from being actuated by heroic and affectionate loyalty to an exiled and suffering race of kings, it is abundantly clear that the great majority were directed by principles just as selfish, and by views just as personal, as ever guided men in the most prudently conducted concerns of business. Under the light of these letters, the ideal gallantry of the Highland chiefs melts into plain, ordinary political selfishness or ambition. But while lairds and lords cut but a poor figure, the character of Duncan Forbes shines out in its true lustre. It is indeed a noble picture of a Scottish patriot that we have here presented to us—one who preferred his country's rights to any party in the State, and who, while acting as the steady friend of government and order, could yet come boldly forward as the earnest and eloquent mediator for his misguided fellow-countrymen, when the punishment proposed seemed to him greater than justice required or their crime deserved. There was no scheme for promoting the welfare, the progress, and the prosperity of the country that did not owe its success to the help of Duncan Forbes. There is no character in Scottish history, from the Revolution to the

Rebellion of 1745, of which Scotsmen of all parties have more reason to be proud. A man of generous and ardent sympathies, a gentleman of stainless reputation and unsullied honour, a patriot pure and disinterested, a statesman of consummate wisdom, of liberal principles, of enlightened understanding, such is Duncan Forbes as we have him revealed to us in the Culloden Papers.

With the exception of some portions of the Culloden Papers, there is a singular dearth of personal testimony as to the events, the sentiments, and the motives of 1745. The histories of Home, Marchant, Boyse, and Henderson, indeed, embody scraps of personal experience and narratives of events by eye-witnesses, but they give little real information of any kind as to the feelings and sentiments prevailing in the country, and least of all any honest contemporary criticism of men and measures. In this respect they are quite colourless, for such was the peculiar temper of the time, that it was not safe to be too plain-spoken on either side. Home's History of the Rebellion is a remarkable instance of this cautious reserve. Impartiality was the professed aim of every writer, but I confess my faith in Mr. Samuel Boyse's "*Impartial* History of the Rebellion" was somewhat shaken by the ominous appearance of the title-page, which contains a flattering portrait of the Duke of Cumberland, with the legend, "Ecce Homo"! And as for Mr. Henderson, his sensitiveness and delicacy render him so susceptible of anything likely to hurt Hanoverian prejudices, that he does not even venture to give the Pretender's name in full when he thinks it would be offensive; and when narrating the scene at Balmerino's execution, he modestly and discreetly veils the awful treason of the stout Earl's last exclamation, by the use of blanks and dashes, thus, "God save K——— J———s and all his R———l F———y"!

It is a relief to turn from such colourless and insipid narratives to the racy pages of the

Chevalier de Johnstone, whose *Memoirs of the Rebellion of 1745* are characterized not only by considerable literary talent, but by candour, impartiality, and shrewd observation. The Chevalier is an outspoken critic, he is never afraid to say boldly and bluntly what he thinks. He had a high opinion of Lord George Murray, and he says so. He had a poor opinion of Prince Charles Edward, and he says so. "Had Prince Charles," he says, "slept during the whole of the expedition, and allowed Lord George Murray to act for him, there is every reason for supposing that he would have found the Crown of Great Britain on his head when he awoke." And again, "All that we can say is, that the Prince entered on this expedition rashly and without foreseeing the personal dangers to which he was about to expose himself; that in carrying it on, he always took care not to expose his person to the fire of the enemy, and that he abandoned it at a time when he had a thousand times more reason to hope for success than when he left Paris to undertake it." For thus daring to express an opinion adverse to the Prince, the Chevalier, who had special opportunities of forming a correct opinion on this point, having acted as aide-de-camp both to the Prince and Lord George Murray, has been called to severe account by such Jacobite writers as Sir Walter Scott, Mr. Robert Chambers, and Lord Mahon.* And because his opinion does not tally with their preconceived ideas of their darling Prince, they have besmirched his fame with foul imputations and done their best to throw discredit upon every statement in his Memoirs. Nevertheless, I think the Chevalier will hold his own as the fairest and ablest critic of the Rebellion of 1745.

I may say in passing, that the Episode of '45 has been singularly rich in chroniclers of a later date. Sir Walter Scott, Mr. Chambers, and Lord Mahon, may be said to have fairly ex-

---

* I have alluded to Earl Stanhope by his older title, because it is the one by which he is best known as a historian; and I have classed him as a Jacobite writer because, whatever his proclivities on other occasions, in his treatment of the Episode of '45 his bias and leaning are too plain to be mistaken.

hausted the subject from a Jacobite point of view. Mr. Chambers's History is the most valuable of these contributions as an antiquarian record, inasmuch as it incorporates and preserves a number of old local and personal traditions which would otherwise most likely have been suffered to die out or become so distorted by oral repetition as to be practically valueless. But the pronounced Jacobite sympathies of all these writers will always render their works liable to the charge of unfair partiality, and will never suffer them to take rank as history. The fact is, that any writer with warm sympathies and a vivid imagination, is in danger of being biassed in favour of Jacobitism, unless he has judgment equal to the control of his feelings. For Jacobitism is peculiarly rich in episodes which appeal to generous and poetic sentiment. It has enlisted all the poets and romancers on its side, and they have done more to falsify history than any amount of patient and honest investigation can ever wholly undo. And I

I

cannot help feeling that it is Mr. Burton's want
of imagination which constitutes his greatest
claim to be listened to with respect and deference
as the historian of this period; whatever his
history for this reason may lack in picturesque-
ness, it gains in fidelity and truthfulness.

But it is time now to turn to by far the most
important branch of the literature of the Jacobite
Episode—its ballads. Never was any period
in the history of any country so rich in this
species of literature as the Jacobite period in
Scottish History. There is no event of any importance, from the Revolution to the battle of
Culloden, which has not its commemorative
ballad, often two or three. Of the adventures
of Charles Edward in 1745 there is not a single
incident, no matter how minute, that has not
been preserved in verse. Every alternation of
hope and despair is chronicled in song. And
the history of the Jacobite Episode may be
traced with far more clearness and minuteness
in this continuous series of ballads than in any

professedly historical work which has ever appeared or probably ever will appear. But this is not the only nor the greatest merit which the Jacobite Ballads possess. They are effusions of real passion—the faithful and graphic expression of emotions which inspired those who composed them, and found an echo in those who listened to them. Moreover, their intrinsic literary excellence as lyrical compositions is not their least remarkable feature. For the Jacobite ballad writers were true poets—they knew how to appeal to the hearts of their hearers in strains which moved pity, or wrath, or laughter, or scorn, or enthusiasm, according as the writer wished the subject to affect those for whom he wrote. And many, perhaps most, of these ballad-writers were of the humblest origin; for there is a depth of romantic and poetical feeling in the lower ranks of the Scottish people, which one would look for in vain amongst the same class in England. And the Jacobites seemed to have enjoyed a monopoly of this poetic sentiment. If the sound principles were all on one side, all the good poetry was on the other; for it would be hard to find more tame and spiritless productions than those of the Whig bards. But wit is generally on the losing side in politics —and the successful ballad is very seldom the accompaniment of the successful cause. This is even more true of the satirical than of the sentimental ballad. It has been well said, that the satirical Muse thrives only in opposition, and the Government which provokes the bitterest satire is generally the most long-lived. All the exquisite poetry, and humour, and invective of the Jacobite Muse were powerless to shake the stability of the Whig monarchy. Yet it would not be correct, on that account, to assume that the influence attributed to this pathetic and satirical literature of Jacobitism has been exaggerated. It was unquestionably a power, and a very effective power, in the country. The memories of Jacobitism, chequered as they were, and with little of glory in them, were full of that pathos and sadness which afford the poet his best subjects, and work more powerfully upon the sympathies and feelings of an imaginative and simple people, than all the achievements of successful renown. It was these ballad-writers who made Jacobitism capable of inspiring that dangerous sentiment of pity, which has done more to bolster up many a weak and worthless cause than the arms of its supporters. And the Jacobite ballads are peculiarly rich in such moving appeals. In the ballads of no other age or country is there to be found so much genuine and touching pathos. It would be impossible to overrate the influence which the wild plaintive minstrelsy, embalming the memories of 1689, 1715, and 1719, had upon the susceptible Celtic nature of the Highlanders. There was a fascination about the new ideas thus associated with the old familiar melodies, which took a strange hold upon the Highland fancy. For the Jacobite minstrels were quick-witted enough to perceive that the

surest way to make their ballads popular, was
to wed them to the music of those beautiful and
simple national airs, which charmed even the
Saxon ear of Dryden. It was fortunate, perhaps, that this influence produced its strongest
effects after the last hope of a successful rebellion had been quenched at Culloden. For the
sixty years which succeeded 1745, Scotland was
more thoroughly Jacobite in her sympathies
than she had ever been when there was a
chance of Jacobitism being successful. There
arose then that romantic, ideal, or sentimental
Jacobitism, of which I have already spoken,
which had no connection with the principles of
the Stuart Government. Indeed, had a restoration been effected, those principles would have
effectually destroyed all the romance with which
the ballad-writers had succeeded in investing a
forlorn and hopeless cause. But, as it was,
there could be no danger in chanting the dirge
of a dead dynasty. All the poetry and romance
of Scotland clustered round Jacobitism. " The

Muses are all Jacobites," said Burns—and his own happiest lyrical efforts, as well as those of Scott, and Hogg, and Cunningham, were inspired by imitation of the ballads of '45.

But it is time to examine some of the features of these Jacobite ballads. It is unfortunate that we have no sure test of the genuineness of a very large number which have been admitted into published collections. For where there is any doubt of their being contemporary effusions, their value, as expressions of popular feeling, is very much lessened. Indeed, their only value is as reflections of the emotions and passions and sentiments of the time when the events to which they refer occurred. We may admire the poetical beauty of the imitations of later writers, for example, some exquisite ballads of Lady Nairn, but they have no historical interest. The Ettrick Shepherd was an indefatigable coiner of these spurious Jacobite ballads, which he palmed off upon the public as genuine productions. There is one admirable song which appeared in his "Jacobite Relics," and which for sly and characteristic Scotch humour is unrivalled,

"Donald's gane up the hill hard and hungry;
Donald comes down the hill wild and angry,"

to which he subjoins this note, "A capital old song, and very popular." And yet will it be believed, the old rascal concocted the song himself, and afterwards, when he was taxed with the offence, admitted it and boasted of it! How many more such spurious ballads and songs may still be passing for genuine, it is impossible to say. But when we find Shenstone's "Jemmy Dawson," and Swift's "Verses on the Union," to say nothing of Campbell's "Lochiel," and no end of songs by Burns, admitted into collections of "Jacobite Ballads," it is impossible to tell when we have got hold of a genuine old Jacobite ballad and when we have got hold of an ingenious imitation. A weeding process is strongly needed, if there were only some one qualified to undertake the task. I hope the publishers of the new edition of Jacobite songs and melodies will endeavour to secure the services of an editor who will set himself honestly to the task of separating the genuine from the spurious.

In the hands of the Ettrick Shepherd, and some other dishonest politicians of his day, the Jacobite ballads were made to serve a political purpose which it would be impossible to censure too harshly. There was a party in the State at that time animated by a rabid hatred of popular principles; they disliked a free and rational government; they would rather have seen a king unfettered by a parliament, a judge unchecked by a jury, and a press free only to praise the stronger side. To promulgate such doctrines openly was not safe; so the advocates of these measures ventilated their views by disguising them under sympathy with and eulogy of the Jacobites, and by stamping with every mark of opprobium and ridicule the great men to whom we owe our present Constitution. Hogg identified himself with this movement, and his

"Jacobite Relics" are disfigured by notes full of personal and political invective.

Such were some of the illegitimate uses which the Ballads were made to serve. Of their legitimate effects in raising a sentimental sympathy with Jacobitism, I have already spoken. There are few, probably, who are not, even at this day, familiar with the effect of a plaintive and pathetic Jacobite song rendered by a woman's voice. It is wonderful what pathos an expressive singer can throw into one of those sweet lyrics bewailing the misfortunes of Charlie. It must be a hard heart that is not melted by the melancholy strain. It must be a dull spirit too that is not kindled into enthusiasm by the martial air and stirring words of "Bonnie Dundee." We feel the effect of such melodies even now—what must they have been when every incident was fresh in the memories of men and women who had felt all the excitement of '15 and '45 ? We can hardly wonder at the effects of such a ballad as "The King shall enjoy his

own again," or "Carle, an' the King come,"
which are said to have done more to re-animate
the hopes of the Stuarts than all the promises
of the French Court, and all their own temporary successes in arms or intrigue.* But I
have often heard it said that, powerful and
telling as these spirited and pathetic ballads are
when they have the advantage of a woman's
sweet voice to give them their most winning
charm, their effect is not to be compared with
that produced by one of the fiercely satirical
ballads, rendered with proper force, and energy,
and emphasis. To hear an old Scottish lawyer,
after his second bottle of port, pour forth the
whole savageness of his soul in the mingled
satire and blasphemy of that wonderfully powerful, but horribly grotesque ballad, "Cumberland
and Murray's Descent into Hell"—

---

* It is only fair, however, to state that there were some ballads produced
on the Whig side, which had an almost equally remarkable effect on popular
feeling. Thomas, Marquis of Wharton, the author of the famous song of
" Lillibulero," used to boast, and not without reason, that with this one song
he had " sung a king out of three kingdoms."

"Ken ye whaur cleekie Murray's gane?
    He's gane to dwell in his lang hame,"

this, I have been told, was something still more characteristic, national, and exciting.

But in considering the influence of these ballads, it must never be forgotten that the object of all such effusions is to distort and exaggerate. They are not to be trusted as strictly faithful pictures of men or manners. Voltaire, speaking of the tendency of such literature in his time, says—" Il y a encore une grande source d'erreurs publiques parmi nous et qui est particulierè à notre nation. C'est le goût des vaudevilles. On en fait chaque jour sur les personnes les plus respectables et on entend tous les jours calomnier les vivans et les morts sur ces beaux fondemens. Ce fait (dit on) est vrai, c'est une chanson qui l'atteste." Voltaire was mistaken, however, in supposing that this was a peculiarity of the French nation, or, if it were so when he wrote, it did not long continue to be. There can be no question that the tendency of these Jacobite ballads, as of all other such compositions, is to burlesque the characters and the events they celebrate. It would be dangerous therefore to accept them as being anything more than indications of the temporary current of popular feeling, while at the same time it would be unwise to disregard them altogether. For, as John Selden sententiously puts it,* "Though some make light of libels (lampoons), yet you may see by them how the wind sits; as take a straw and throw it up into the air, you shall see by that which way the wind is, which you shall not do by casting up a stone. More solid things do not show the complexion of the times so well as ballads and libels." It has been urged against Lord Macaulay, that he has carried this theory to excess. "Give Macaulay,† says a recent writer, "an insulated fact or phrase, a scrap of a journal, or the tag end of a song, and on it, by the abused prerogative of genius, he would construct a theory of national or personal char-

---

* Selden, "Table-Talk." † Paget, "New Examen."

acter which should confer undying glory or inflict indelible disgrace." And indeed so frequent is this habit with Macaulay, that it has added greatly to that general distrust of his accuracy and impartiality which has been steadily growing among historical critics, and will soon oust him from the place he now falsely holds as a faithful and truthful historian. It is safer and wiser therefore to accept Voltaire's maxim rather than Selden's.

Any statement of the influence and effects of Jacobite literature upon Scotland would be incomplete without an acknowledgement of the work done in this direction by the author of "Waverley." It is of course impossible for us now to appreciate that remarkable novel as it was appreciated sixty years ago, when there were persons still living who had spoken with fugitives from Culloden, and had heard the rebellion discussed at many a fireside by those who had a deep personal interest in the rebels. It is still, and must have been more then, the charm of "Waverley," that its characters and descriptions are vivid and lifelike, drawn from living originals. This was the cause of its marvellous popularity. And it is fortunate for literature that the national feeling was caught up and impersonated while there was yet something of it alive to warm the sympathies of the novelist. But "Waverley" had a twofold influence. Jacobitism had so long been a tabooed subject, kept out of sight as a thing fraught with some mysterious danger to the Constitution, that people were startled to find that it was now a matter of history—that it need no longer be banished from contemplation, but might be freely discussed and sympathized with, without any fear of consequences. Sir Walter Scott first roused English people to the conviction that Jacobitism was a harmless memory of the past, and it at once became the fashion. Here was a romance in their very midst which they had all this while been neglecting. The rest is well known. The Highlands swarmed with pilgrims eager to pay their tribute of admiration at the shrine of Charles Edward and Flora MacDonald. From that time friendlier feelings sprang up between Scotchmen and Englishmen, for they had one common object of admiration. From that time, too, a closer and more cordial relationship arose between Lowlanders and Highlanders. They discovered that they possessed cherished memories in common, that they were sons of the same dear mother-land, and that the name and fame of Scotland were as dear to the one as to the other.

" Thus the whirligig of Time brings in his revenges." The Union, which was the *bête noir* of one party, and Jacobitism, which was the *bête noir* of the other, have both had their share in making Scotland what she is, a rich, prosperous, happy, and independent country. We have lived to see the royal descendant of George I. build herself a stately mansion in the very heart of those Highlands which were the dreaded home of Jacobitism, but which she now loves better than the Herrenhausen, better than her noblest English palace, and where she is loved with an affection as sincere, and served with a loyalty as devoted, as were ever vouchsafed even to " Bonnie Prince Charlie."

THE

Jacobite Episode in Scottish History

AND

ITS RELATIVE LITERATURE.

AN ESSAY

BY

J. LOGIE ROBERTSON, M.A.

EDINBURGH.

"Give me the making of a country's songs, and let who will make its laws."

JOHN MENZIES & COMPANY,
EDINBURGH & GLASGOW.
SIMPKIN, MARSHALL, & COMPANY,
LONDON.

THE

Jacobite Episode in Scottish History

AND ITS

RELATIVE LITERATURE.

"Give me the making of a country's songs, and let who will make its laws."

THE Jacobite Episode in Scottish History ex-
tends over a period of about sixty years,—from
1688 to 1746. Within these limits is confined
the actual struggle of a party devotedly attached
to the declining House of Stuart, and bitterly
opposed to the introduction of an alien dynasty.
It was a period of great agitation, affecting more
or less every individual in the country, and kept
alive by the very varying fortunes which now
gladdened with hopes, and now embittered with
losses, the parties engaged in the struggle.
Indeed, so sharp was the conflict, and waged

K

with such determined animosity on both sides, that it would have been impossible for a passive spectator to predict the ultimate issue, and it even now surprises the reader of Scottish history to find that matters terminated as they did. The Stuart or Jacobite party lost when they were apparently on the eve of winning: their hopes, frequently dimmed, never extinguished, seemed, perhaps,—on a general survey of the events of the period within which the actual struggle was pent,—to become brighter according as the struggle enlarged its area, thus demanding a closer and more numerous attention, and in proportion as it continued its course, thus exciting a determination to end it, and an absorbing interest as to how it would end. And it was just when the expectations of the losing side appeared on the point of realization, that they suffered a full and final eclipse.

But, apart altogether from the excitement of the struggle as consequent upon the various phases through which it passed, there were certain elements in the struggle, from its very commencement, when it was as yet only prospective, that tended to create an all-engrossing interest in the national mind. The subject of dispute was one in which there could hardly be any neutrals. One of two sides must be taken, and a compromise was impossible. The divisional line between the two parties was clear and well defined. It was not made merely on ecclesiastical grounds, on political grounds, or on individual grounds. That is too narrow a view to take of the question upon the settlement of which a whole nation split. No doubt these various grounds of differences had their influence in deepening the rancour of the conflicting parties. But the prime question of difference was,—Are we to have a Stuart to reign over us? It was, in other words, Jacobitism or Non-Jacobitism. And from this, the original or central question in dispute, sprung other differences, based upon the character, religion, and political measures of the unfortunate sovereign in whose reign the seeds of revolution were sown. These smaller differences centred in the primal one, and affected it in various ways. They were not all ranged on the same side. So that it is not strictly correct to regard the wars that sprang up around the question of Jacobitism or Non-Jacobitism, as being waged between Papists and Protestants, Tories and Whigs, or adherents to the persons of the Stuarts and those that were not so. Papists and Protestants were found on the same side,— in very different proportions, it is true; Whigs and Tories were banded together against Whigs and Tories; and those that had no love or respect for the person of James II., or of his son, "the Pretender," leagued with those that had. In short, the prime question, the settlement of which occasioned the long and persistent sixty years' struggle, must be regarded in its broadest feature as one involving an abstract idea of right. And this idea may be stated thus,—the regal jurisdiction of the country is at all times the right of the direct lineal descendant of the last hereditary monarch. This idea is everywhere familiar in the famous expression—*the divine right of kings.* It is the same idea which the poet chieftain of Strowan has thrown into verse—

> " The laws of God and man declare
> The son should be the father's heir."

This, then, was the great argument of the Jacobite party; and it is evident that it admits of only one answer, belief or denial. In the settlement of the question, which its enunciation demanded of every intelligent person, the nation was divided almost to a man. Every individual was to decide for himself; neutral party there could not well be. In the decision of the question, however, there were naturally many whose minds were influenced by the character, manners, beliefs religious and political, conduct, and even personal appearance of the sovereign in whose reign the question was propounded, and of his opponent, the head of the party who denied the divine right of kings, and advocated parliamentary government.

In this way the struggle was one of very mixed elements. And the apparently incongruous mixture for the most part added fury to both sides. There were, no doubt, persons who believed in the doctrine of hereditary right, and who, nominally at least, sided with the Jacobite party, and who yet viewed with disgust the papistical and despotic tendencies of the sovereign to whom they believed they justly owed allegiance. Such men could bring only half of their hearts to the Jacobite side, and by their cold and reluctant proffer of service exert a deterrent or damping influence upon others who looked to them for example. But many of these could ill bear the unsatisfactory position of one who is only half pledged to the party among whose ranks he nominally arrays himself. They either allowed the grand idea of divine right to swallow up every other consideration, and then lent their weight to the cause of Jacobitism; or they were driven to Jacobitism, and entirely committed to it, heart and body, by the taunts of "renegade" or "apostate," flung at them by their political or ecclesiastical confrères of the non-Jacobite ranks. We do find that such was the case: we find that Tory and Papist were employed synonymously with Jacobite in the heat and din of the struggle; but it must not be forgotten that there were true Protestants and honest Whigs on both sides, and that the prime division of the country was by vote on the question,—king hereditary or king parliamentary?

From this brief glance of the struggle in its origin and in its progress, it will be evident how complete and fierce the agitation of the nation was. The extent and thoroughness of the agitation, however, can be fully measured and estimated only by a reference to the contemporaneous literature that sprang up amidst the storm of the Jacobite dissensions. The period of active Jacobitism was one of warfare, not merely of swords but of pens; and the influence of the latter in giving edge and weight to the former must not be forgotten. Confining our attention, meanwhile, to the literature of the time as bearing upon the extent and nature of the agitation in the country, we observe, as the first thing to catch our notice, the enormous quantity of it, and its exclusively controversial and satirical character in both prose and verse. Its voluminousness is a remarkable feature, and in itself indicates the absorbing interest of the questions which required such extensive discussion. It would appear that the mind of the nation had been so roused and concentrated upon one idea,—the idea of Jacobitism *pro* and *con*,—that the consideration of every other topic foreign to this was firmly excluded. The stream of Scottish Literature, which first began to sparkle out so unmistakeably in the time of John Barbour, which gained such accessions of strength and volume in the age of William Dunbar and David Lindsay, and which was still further increased by the nameless but romanti-

cally beautiful tributaries of later ballads and
songs, would seem about this time to have
been stayed, dammed up, or turned aside. It
was untasted by the generation of the early part
of the eighteenth century. That generation
dug out a literature for themselves,—a big
muddy pool, with, however, many clear freshets,
somewhere near the main stream and only in
trickling contact with it. In other words, the
period in Scotland from about 1688 to 1746 was
not a time fitted for the production or the study
of pure literature. That requires leisure and
fastidious pruning. This was a time of action,
—of unpremeditated thought and impulsive
word. It was a time of business. There was
no holiday in which to while away the hours in
the study of past literatures, or in the deliberate
planning and leisurely executing of some carefully chosen literary subject. The blood was
coursing too fast through the heart of the nation
to admit of either contemplative study or refined
production. Things had to be said and done

quickly, and there was hardly room for thought. Yet the pen was too influential an instrument to be left lying neglectedly, as if it were only designed for peaceful scenes and gala days. It had already done good work,—palpable work, for Scotland, in the pamphleteering days of the Charleses. Its aid was therefore required, and it was used without stint; and often, very often, to chronicle the fierce thought newly-sprung in the heart, in both ecclesiastical pamphlet and satirical ballad.

Satirical literature flourishes in times of debate and dissension, and is then always personal. From this circumstance, and the fact that the literature of Jacobitism is enormously large, important conclusions may be deduced.

It is with communities as it is with individuals. The former are aggregates of the latter. Both have characters, and the characters of both may be read in the same way. We read the character of an individual in private life by his conversation and conduct; an author's book furnishes us with a key to his character; and by its literature we look into the character of a community, a nation, or a period. It must be premised here,—and it is an admission that all will allow,—that a man's character is formed by what most continuously and constantly occupies his thoughts; and that whatever a man thinks most about, he must speak most about. If this be true of an individual in a general way, it is much more worthy of reliance when spoken of as regards a community. For a community is less capable of playing the impostor than an individual: it is composed of elements that act less harmoniously, less in concert with each other than the mental faculties of an individual may; and is, therefore, as it were, unavoidably compelled honestly to reveal its character.

The chances of being able correctly and readily to read the character of a community are much increased when the prevailing form of its literature is the satirical. This is obvious. Satire begets satire. It is personal in its attacks and in its replies. We thus hear both sides, and so can form a tolerably correct opinion. At the same time, it is often unsparing in its revelation of its author's own character. In his satire the author not seldom shews his own weaknesses, meannesses, passions, feelings, hopes, resolutions. His exposure of the enemy against whom he has levelled his satire may be incorrect,—of himself it is not so. A man is in earnest when he is angry; and the angry satiric muse reveals at once his anger and his earnestness,—in other words, his character.

But further, it has been said that what an author thinks most about, he must write most about; and *vice versâ*. As in the voluminousness, therefore, of an author's works, so in that of the literature of a community, we have another means of arriving at a correct notion of its character.

Now, the literature born of Jacobitism is a well-defined one, wholly cut off from, and untinged by antecedent literatures; it is, further, in a very marked degree the offspring of contemporary events, and, to use an expressive phrase, "bristling" with personal allusions; and, in the third place, it is very voluminous,—indeed so much so, even in the department of poetry, that hundreds of the ballads which it so largely includes have been neglected by enthusiastic collectors.

The Jacobite Episode in Scottish History is thus abundantly and faithfully mirrored in the Satirical Songs and ballads which appeared contemporaneously with the persons and events of which they treat. We may, therefore, study Jacobitism through the medium of these ballads.

It would be no very difficult matter to arrange the Jacobite ballads in chronological order. From the freshness and minuteness of detail with which they chronicle the passing events to which they allude, one would be at little loss to set them in their proper sequence of production, although the authors are mostly unknown and no date is affixed to any of them. Indeed, so full are they of historical allusions, that a very complete narrative of the main features, and many of the minor details, of the great Jacobite struggle can be gathered from their perusal. They are most numerous and interesting at those central points in the course of the struggle, around which Jacobitism was naturally at its fullest activity. These central points are the Accession of the Prince of Orange, the Battle of Killiecrankie, the Glencoe Butchery, the Darien Expedition, the Death of William III., the Act of Succession, the Union, the Coronation of George I., "the Fifteen," and "the Forty-five," with their accompanying circumstances respectively. A noticeable feature in the narrative of the events of the Jacobite episode, as told directly or incidentally in the Jacobite ballads, is the absence of all abuse on the part of the metrical satirists in connexion with the names of Queen Mary and Queen Anne. The name of the latter is frequently mentioned, but never in the vituperative style which the writers assume when dealing with William and the Georges: she is warned, and described in a satirically familiar strain, but there are no gross allusions or coarse exaggerations of a personal or social nature, which the writers knew well how to fabricate when speaking of the male sovereigns who occupied the abdicated Stuart throne. . Mary is scarcely, if ever, mentioned. Whether the Jacobites had adopted the motto of making no war against women, or whether they tolerated the sovereignty of Queen Mary and Queen Anne as being more nearly related to the exiled House, it is difficult to judge,—and, probably, both reasons influenced them to forbearance.

The narrative of the struggle, as gleaned from the Jacobite songs and ballads, is briefly as follows: The Revolution was quietly accomplished in Scotland, partly owing to the skill with which the welcomers of the Prince of Orange had laid their plans, and partly owing to the total want of Jacobite activity in England. Notwith-

standing the absence of any opposition, however, when William was proclaimed King he
was acknowledged liege lord by only a faction
in Scotland.   There were scattered throughout
the country smouldering embers of discord,
which awaited only the breath of the Viscount
of Dundee to fan them into a blaze.   This man,
of whose character we have such conflicting
accounts, was at least fearless and energetic in
the cause he had adopted.   He is the central
figure in the early part of the Jacobite struggle.
By the force of his own genius he drew around
him a body of devoted Highlanders, whose
espousal of the Jacobite interest is an anomaly
requiring explanation.   The main body of
Highlanders who gathered around him followed
the command and example of their chieftains,
and these were influenced in favour of the
exiled House by at least two considerations:
in the first place, Argyll, the personal foe of
many of them, was an adherent of the Prince of
Orange, whose establishment on the throne

would restore the power, territorial and political, which Argyll had lost in the preceding reign; and this return of power would be at their cost and to their danger. In the second place, the policy of the Prince of Orange, manifest from the first, was to promote peace and commerce in the country by the suppression of the danger- ous feudal power held by the chieftains, and by an equable and rigid administration of the laws throughout the entire country. This was the aiming of a blow, likely to prove fatal, at that warlike mode of life, prevalent in the Highlands from time immemorial, by which the clans maintained their existence. Peace and commerce were inimical to those whose lives were spent in feuds and maraudings, and whose constant and almost sole profession was that of arms. Conscious of this, conscious also of his own adaptive and inspiring genius, and with the great name of Montrose to conjure by, Dundee had little difficulty in raising a sufficient body of Highlanders, at the head of whom he met

L

Mackay, the general commissioned by the Scottish Convention to frustrate his plans. The battle of Killiecrankie ensued,—a complete victory to the Jacobite cause, but without any except a momentary significance, as Dundee fell in the action.

We gather from the various ballads descriptive of this engagement many interesting historical details. First of all, there is noted the superior position occupied by the Highlanders, and the difficulty experienced by Mackay's troops in charging uphill the descending foe:

> " Clavers and his highlandmen
>   Came down upon the raw;"

and

> " The Solemn League and Covenant
>   Came *whigging* up the hills."

The activity of the clansmen is struck off in the verse,—

> " O'er bush, o'er bank, o'er ditch, o'er stank,
>   *She* flang amang them a'."

It was a hand-to-hand conflict, such as the " durk "-armed clansmen loved,—favourable for the display of individual exploits. The "bauld Pitcur"—"*Pitcurius heroicus Hector Scoticanus*" —is especially celebrated for his deeds of daring. On the winning side, however, there were cravens. A body of Irish auxiliaries, in the uniform of the deposed King James, fled to the hills while the battle was raging. They are not spared by the Jacobite satirist. Hanging, in his opinion, would be too good for them; for, if they had "bent their brows" like the Scottish Celts,—an allusion to the fierce determination with which the Higlanders are wont to rush to the onset,—they would have "saved their king" and compelled the flight of William. But there were cravens, too, among the troops of Mackay; and the Scottish metrical satirist is especially derisive on the hare-heartedness of the "Mogan Dutch," when "Maclean and his fierce men came in amang them a'." Satire, however, is not always truthful, and must not be taken as affording a correct account of the subject of its play. Conscious, or unconscious of the falsity of his statement,—and, perhaps, as much the latter as the former in the turbid times in which he wrote,—the contemporary Jacobite satirist of the battle of Killiecrankie accuses Mackay of personal cowardice during the engagement: " O fie, Mackay," he says,

> "What gart ye lie
> I' the bush ayont the brankie?"

Mackay's honour as a brave and skilful general requires no advocacy. At the same time, it may be quite true that he kept out of the mêlée of the fight; but this conduct, as the commanding officer, he was not only warranted but obliged by a sense of duty to adopt.

On the death of Dundee, General Cannon was commissioned by King James to maintain his cause in Scotland. Never was more unhappy choice of a commander made. He lacked the genius of his predecessor in dealing with the fiery-spirited Gaels. His camp was a scene of almost uninterrupted insubordination. The chieftains quarrelled with him and with each other, and daily left his diminishing army. The final disaster was at Cromdale, where he allowed himself to be entrapped and surprised in bed. The Jacobite cause was not again supported in Scottish field till a quarter of a century had passed.

About two months after the affair at Cromdale, the battle of the Boyne was fought in Ireland. King William's departure from England to assert his supremacy in Ireland is described in one of the ballads. He is styled "Willie Wanbeard," and is depicted as setting forth on his expedition armed with a "boortree" gun and a "shabble," and as conducting himself on the voyage in a most undignified way through an attack of sea-sickness. The war in Ireland, it is well known, was prolonged for a year after the defeat of James's army at the Boyne; and to support his claims under this reverse, their own leader being dead, several Scottish Jacobite gentlemen who had fought at Killiecrankie now volunteered their services on Irish soil.

Disaster still attended the arms of the Jacobites in Ireland; and, on the capitulation of Limerick, they chose to go into a voluntary exile with their master, rather than enjoy the comforts of peace and domestic happiness in their native land. This chivalric behaviour is referred to in the ballad :—

> " It was a' for our richtfu' king
> We left fair Scotland's strand,
> It was a' for our richtfu' king
> We e'er saw Irish land ; "

And,

> " He turned him richt an' round about
> Upon the Irish shore ;
> An' ga'e his bridle-reins a shake,
> With, Adieu for evermore ! "

Nothing in the whole history of Jacobitism can more forcibly illustrate the devotion and fidelity which marked the adherence of the Stuart party to the side of hereditary monarchy, than the conduct of these gentlemen,—upwards of a hundred in number, and by far the majority of them Protestants,—in cheerfully exposing themselves to the hardships of exile, foreign service, scanty means, loss of social position, starvation, sickness, and even death;—and all this, that they might not be better off than their master, and might not be chargeable to his foreign friends.

In the lull of the Jacobite storm, which followed the defeat and dispersion of the Highlanders among the "Haughs" of Cromdale, government was taking active steps for the preservation of peace in Scotland. In 1690, the clans were broken up, the oath of allegiance from the chieftains enforced, forts established in the Highlands, and a system of espionage organized throughout the country. These measures, while they still further weakened the power of the Highlanders, increased the hatred of the Jacobites against the prevailing government; and then, as if to fill the cup of their wrath to the brim, came the Massacre of Glencoe and the disasters of the attempted Scottish colonization of Darien. These calamities evoked throughout the length and breadth of Scotland the bitterest expressions of aversion and hatred to the person of King William. Even the Lowland Whigs, most of whom were well-affected towards the sovereignty of the Prince of Orange, gave utterance to their displeasure and discontent in threats and ex-ecrations,—for both the calamities were viewed as national, the unfortunate affair of Darien particularly rankling in the breasts of the peace-fully-inclined trading Lowlanders. The death of the king was accordingly the signal for a jubilant outburst of Jacobite feeling. The mole, as the remote agent of his death, was toasted as "the little gentleman in the velvet coat." In the satirical ballad of this date (1702), entitled "Willie Winkie's Testament," the king is represented as being afraid to face death with the memory of Glencoe and Darien on his conscience. Father Tennison is his confessor, receiving his last words at his bedside, and is being implored by the despairing monarch in broken English to remove from his mind the recollection of

> " All de curses of de Scot,
> Dat dey did give me wonder vell
> For Darien and dat Macdonell.
> O take dem off mine hands, I pray!
> I'll go de lighter on my vay."

He is further figured as being desirous of cooping up the Scots within their own country, excluding them from the privileges enjoyed by the English in matters social and commercial, and cramping all their efforts of national development and colonial enterprise. It will annoy and vex him, even in his grave, to learn that they are a successful and flourishing people:

> " Keep de Scot beyond de Tweed,
> Else I shall see dem ven I'm dead."

In another party-song of the same period, William is erroneously charged with having urged on to his ruin the young Duke of Monmouth, who suffered for rebellion early in the reign of James II. He is accused of flattery, falseness, and duplicity in the matter of Monmouth's death,—

> "Wi' the waggin' o' his fause tongue
> He gart the brave Monmouth dee."

But this charge is quite devoid of proof. It was, however, apparently the prevailing opinion among the disaffected, and would doubtless tend still further to give emphasis to the current expression in which they spoke of him as "a *fause* an' a foreign loon."

All through the latter half of King William's reign and the whole of Queen Anne's, the Jacobite party expended their activity in toasting the exiled family, circulating bad reports of Whiggish government, and above all, in endeavouring to turn the popular feeling into Jacobite channels by means of pamphlets and songs; while their leaders exerted their utmost in striving to oust from places of influence in the State their Whig opponents, or in plotting and caballing in secret. In these attempts they were for the most part unsuccessful, yet always

encouraged to increased exertion by the tempt-
ing nearness to success to which they sometimes
attained. An undoubted success was at last
deemed to have been achieved when, in 1704,
the Act of Succession was, as the poet of the
event describes it, "kicked out by a vote" in
the Scottish parliament. This result was
brought about by a coalition of parties. The
cementing bond of union between them was the
common determination to have the same commercial privileges extended to Scotland which
obtained in England, or to be an independent community and have a sovereign of their
own. This *Act of Security*, as it was called,
was the outward and palpable expression of
the national discontent with respect to the
Darien failure. It gave unbounded joy to the
Scottish Jacobites, who now began to anticipate
the return of the Stuarts to their ancient kingdom of Scotland. The time was ardently looked
forward to "when the king should come o'er
the water"; and many an earnest prayer was

prayed for life to be prolonged to see the day
when "the king should enjoy his own again."
Heaven was implored to send propitious gales
to hasten his glad approach. But whatever
inclemencies of weather should intervene, only
let him at least be restored, they prayed, to the
love and loyalty of his devoted subjects:

> " Then blaw ye east, or blaw ye west,
>   Or blaw ye ower the faem,—
>   O bring the lad that I lo'e best,
>   And ane I daurna name!"

Shortly after this, the tone of the Jacobites is
changed to one of lamentation. The Union of
the Parliaments was accomplished in 1707.
The strain is now,—

> " Fareweel to a' our Scottish fame,
>   Fareweel our ancient glory,
>   Fareweel ev'n to the Scottish name
>   Sae fam'd in martial story!"

The nation is spoken of as having been "sold."
The transfer of the national rights is attributed
to "a parcel of rogues." The "rogues" are all
mentioned, and wickedly satirized in the ballad

of the *Awkward Squad.* They are called deceivers, turn-coats, traitors, and worse. The satire is especially bitter against the Earl of Stair. He is styled a vulture to his country; and all the evils that, in the Jacobite estimation, ever befell Scotland since the Revolution, are attributed to him. He was the prime instigator of the massacre of the poor Macdonalds; and now, by his influence in procuring the Union, he has sold his country for gold. In another satire on the same subject, Stair is alluded to as the "wonderful" bridegroom to whom Scotland is to be unwillingly wedded. Among other names conspicuous in the ballads about the Union, that of the Earl of Mar is held up to public scorn.

The Jacobites, however, were not quite dispirited. They had sent for the Chevalier Saint George, the son of the late dethroned monarch, in whom their hopes and wishes now centred. He was then residing at Paris, acknowledged by the French sovereign as the king of Great Britain, and waiting for a fit opportunity of stretching forth his arm to claim his rights. He was spoken of by the Government party as " The Pretender," from the circumstance that, at his birth, the absurd idea of a spurious origin was circulated throughout the country. Amply provided by the French king with arms, ammunition, money, and a fleet, he set out for the ancient kingdom of his ancestors, and arrived in the Firth of Forth just a couple of days after the appearance in the same firth of the English squadron sent to defend the coasts. He avoided an engagement, and coasting northwards attempted a landing at Inverness. Contrary winds, however, were against him, and he was driven back to France. And thus ended disastrously an attempt which, if it had been undertaken in favourable weather, would have secured a landing, and without doubt the possession of at least Scotland.

The latter half of Queen Anne's reign was a period of intense excitement to the Jacobite party. Pamphlets and satirical songs were rife, and fomented the ever-growing excitement. The queen herself was never abusively handled in these popular satires, we have seen; on the contrary, there are occasional references which seem to point to the fact of the queen being herself a Jacobite. It was believed she was at heart a Tory; it was whispered that she had given audiences to the Chevalier; it is certain that latterly in her reign the Tories were in possession of nearly all influential offices of state, and that just a week before her death they had prepared a plan which would deprive every Whig in the country of situations of trust and power, as well in the army as at the court. Her sudden death, however, paralyzed their plans; indecision marked the policy of the leading Jacobites at court; the Whigs acted with promptness and vigour, and, before the Jacobites had time to oppose an effectual resistance, the Elector of Hanover was in London. He had accepted with alacrity a crown which he hardly expected ever to wear. He is represented in the famous ballad of *The*

Wee German Lairdie as quite absorbed in the petty matters of his own quiet principality, and scarcely troubling his mind, since the death of his mother Sophia, about matters in Great Britain:

> "When we gaed to bring him hame,
> He was delvin in his kail-yardie."

A great deal of talking and resolving was indulged in, especially in England, on the accession of the Hanoverian prince. In Scotland the people were not so demonstrative, but more determined upon action. They were still greatly dissatified with the Union: it was a national grievance, indeed; and of this fact the Jacobites were not slow to avail themselves in fomenting a rebellion. As the Jacobite feeling became hotter, it became more national, more Scottish; it sought to identify Jacobitism with the preservation of the ancient realm of the Jameses. There began to be manifested a tendency to revive the old historical feelings of jealousy and enmity towards England. The national memory, in the songs of this date, is pointed backwards to the times of Wallace and the Bruce. The past glories of the country are made to live again:

> "See Edward, their king, take his heels in a flight,
>   Nor e'er look behind, but in Berwick alight;
>   In an old fishing-boat he bade Scotland good-night,—
>   O the broad swords," &c.

And now England must be met with the same determined valour in her state attempts to annihilate Scotland. Scotland must regain her independence. And the combined causes of national independence and hereditary monarchy are artfully interwoven:

> "Our king they do despise
>   Because of Scottish blood;
>   But ere Brunswick sceptre wield,
>   We'll do or die in field,
>   But never never yield
>   To serve a foreign brood."

This tendency, however, to make the struggle a national one was not general to the country. It occasionally cropped up, but only among the ranks of the extreme Jacobites; and is to be

M

regarded as the expression of their willingness to see the industries of the country they loved so well injured and ruined, its strength over-matched, and its independence risked, rather than witness the old Scottish coronation-chair filled by other than a Stuart.

To combine the scattered energies of the Jacobites, there came down from London, whence he had been driven by the coldness, suspicion, and actual aversion manifested towards him by the newly-crowned king, the unscrupulous but skilful and ambitious Earl of Mar. He came down to Scotland with nearly half a million of pounds, which he had been most expeditious in collecting, and after he had concerted measures with certain Jacobite leaders for a rising on the Borders to take place simultaneously with his own projected gathering of the Highland clans. The object of Mar's errand to Scotland was not long in spreading over the land. It was hailed with exuberant delight by every honest Jacobite; and Mar's participation in the framing of the detested Union, as explained by himself, was overlooked or forgotten. Great achievements were predicted from his movements in the Highlands. Success appeared to be still within grasp. Accordingly we find the songs of the period even more plentiful, and more daringly outspoken in their language, from anticipated victory, than any that had yet appeared. The person, character, and past life of King George, are keenly and unsparingly assailed. He is charged with the crime of murder:

> " At hame, in Hanóver, he killed in cold blood,
>   A pretty young Swede,"—

an accusation which was substantially true. He is pictured as a coarse profligate, addicted to the open indulgence of the most sensual vices. He is described as " a pilfering bandit." In his *Testament*, part of his wardrobe is thus catalogued,—

> " Ane auld black coat, baith lang an' wide,
>   Wi' snishen barken'd like a hide,
>   A *skeplet* hat, and plaiden hose,
>   A jerkin clarted a' wi' brose."

And so on, in satirical strains that, while they confessedly caricature, at the same time utterly *un*king the subject of their attack.

There is further proof of the anticipated success cherished by the Jacobites, in the tone of perfect security and carelessness with which, about this time, they published their treasonable ideas. A song of this date, which appears to have been eminently popular in its day, thus boldly breaks out,—

> " Come, let us drink a health, boys,
>   A health unto our king;
> We'll drink no more by stealth, boys,
>   Come, let our glasses ring;
> For England must surrender,
> To him they call Pretender;
> God save our faith's defender,
>   And our true lawful king."

The work of the Earl of Mar in behalf of the exiled Stuarts, and his raising of the clans, are kept no secret. " Hey for Bobbing John," goes one of the songs, alluding to Mar,

> " And his Highland quorum ! . . .

> Many a sword and lance
>   Swings at Highland hurdie;
> How they'll skip and dance
>   O'er the bum o' Geordie!"

Far from making the rebellion a secret, the Jacobites even challenge the Government party to a trial of strength:

> " But wad ye come, or daur ye come,
>   Afore the bagpipe an' the drum,
> We'll either gar ye a' sing dumb,
>   Or 'Auld Stuarts back again.'"

Still further to raise the Jacobite hopes of success, the fruit of an alliance with the famous Charles XII. of Sweden, came in the shape of a promise of aid in men and ammunition; and even the "mysterious" Czar,—as reads the ballad in which both he and the "valiant Swede" are toasted,—is expected to assist in the restoration of the "Auld Stuarts."

The plan which Mar had selected for the gathering of the clans was the then common pretext of a hunting-match. Accordingly, there met at Braemar all the disaffected noblemen and gentlemen whom the Earl had taken care to invite, and thus was obtained an opportunity of planning in concert for the overthrow of the Guelph dynasty. Among those who were present at this gathering, the ballads particularly mention the Marquises of Huntly and Tullibardine; the Earls of Southesk, Errol, Traquair, and Seaforth; Viscounts Kilsyth and Kenmure; Lords Rollo, Strathallan, Nairne, and Oliphant; and among the Highland chieftains, Glengarry, Glenderule, and Auldubair,—besides very many others of various ranks and conditions. It was resolved by the assembled Jacobite chiefs to take the field. The Chevalier was expected soon to arrive, and, in the meantime, preparations went on. The Highlands were traversed by bodies of armed men, " plaided and plumed," and all marching to the warlike strains of the bagpipe, from various quarters to the central rallying point of Braemar. *The Chevalier's Muster-Roll* enumerates many of the clans that made their appearance in answer to the summons of Mar. The numbers continued to increase till fully ten thousand men were in the field. The standard of rebellion was then flung abroad on the mountain breezes, but an ominous event happened at the ceremony, which appears to have been remembered by the more superstitious of the Jacobites. The event is celebrated in the lines of the song,—

> " But when our standard was set up,
>   So fierce the wind did blaw,
> The golden knop down from the top
>   Unto the ground did fa'."

Government, meanwhile, was not idle. The Duke of Argyll was in Scotland, and rousing his clansmen and the Lowland Whigs to a sense of their danger. Unaided almost, he managed to collect an army of about three thousand, and secured a strong position of watch and defence at Stirling. Mar, long delaying to strike the blow for which he was so well prepared, was now in the neighbourhood of Sheriffmuir, waiting for the co-operation from the south of

Viscount Kenmure and the Earl of Derwent-water, and for the arrival of the Chevalier to head the campaign. His want of despatch, which allowed Argyll to seize the gate between the Highlands and the Lowlands; his ignorance of the clansmen, whose courage rose with activity and fell proportionately with inaction; his cowardice, which prevented him from facing an army trebly outnumbered by his own; and his total incapacity to manœuvre large bodies of men in the field,—all combined to produce the disgraceful check which he sustained on Sheriff-muir, and which virtually quelled the rebellion for thirty years.

The Jacobite satirists did not spare the pusillanimity of certain of the rebel chiefs on this occasion:

" Whether we ran or they ran, or we wan or they wan,
    Or if there was winnin' at a',
  There's no man can tell, save our brave general,
    Who first began rinnin' at a'."

The ballads of the period describe the battle

with great minuteness, and with remarkable fairness to both sides. Those individuals who showed courage on either side are impartially commended, and the cowardice and flight of others are as faithfully ridiculed. The Marquis of Huntly is especially unfortunate in having fallen into the hands of a rhyming satirist whose sympathies are evidently with the Grants, the hereditary rivals of the Gordons. We must regard *From Bogie Side* or *The Marquis' Raide* as the song of a rival clan glad of an opportunity to accuse their neighbours of a dishonourable defeat, and greatly magnifying it in the accusation. There appears to have been decided cowardice, however, in the precipitate flight of Huntly from the battle-field. It is alluded to in various songs of the times, besides occupying a prominent place in the satirical ballad of *From Bogie Side*. In the lament of *O my King*, the writer exclaims,—" I would not be in Huntly's case, for honours, lands, an' a';" and, in a succeeding verse, he is openly charged with having betrayed the Stuart cause, not so much out of cowardice as out of treachery. Seaforth is included in the charge; and, although the general tone of the lament is one of sad denunciation of the conduct of the renegade lords, yet the writer cannot deny himself the luxury of an occasional satirical sting:

> " I wish these lords had stay'd at hame
> And milked their minnie's ewes."

A remarkable feature of the battle was the total rout of the left wing on both sides. Hence arose those conflicting rumours of the issue of the conflict which prevailed for some time after the engagement was over, and which are embodied in the contemporaneous metrical descriptions of the battle. The "chase" is at one time represented as having gone to the north, or Perth-ward,—at another time as having gone to the south, or Stirling-ward. Both accounts are true, and easily reconcileable. The flight of the left wing of Mar's forces is attributed to the treachery of one Lawrence Drummond,—a spy in the pay of Argyll and acting as *aid de camp* to Mar,—who galloped to Hamilton, the commander of the left wing of the insurgents, with orders contrary to what he had received from the generalissimo. Mar's instructions were to attack instantly and with vigour, as the right wing had already encountered the enemy and were achieving a victory. The order delivered by the *aid de camp* was to withdraw, as defeat appeared to be impending. By the delivery of this order a panic was created in the ranks of the insurgent left, and when the enemy pressed them they fled ignominiously from the field. Drummond, subsequently in the day, crossed over to the side of Argyll. His conduct is severely exposed and condemned by the song-writers of the day:

" Then Lawrie the traitor, who betray'd his master,
    His King, and his country, an' a',
  Pretending Mar might give orders to fight—(flight?)
    To the right of the army awa'.
  Then Lawrie, for fear of what he might hear,
    Took Drummond's best horse, and awa';
  'Stead o' going to Perth he crossed the firth,
    Alongst Stirling bridge and awa';

To London he pressed, and there he professed
 That he behaved best o' them a';
An' so, without strife, got settled for life,—
 A hundred a year to his fa'.
In Borroustounness he resides with disgrace
 Till his neck stand in need o' a thraw;
An' then in a tether he'll swing frae a ledder,
 An' go aff the stage with applau'."

Carnegie of Phinaven is satirized in the same songs, despite the activity and enterprize he had shewn on former occasions in rousing his countrymen, at Amalree and elsewhere, in favour of the Jacobite interests. He is described as possessing the genius of an excellent recruiting officer, but as being totally unqualified for the position of a fighting officer. In the disguise of a piper, and relying upon the Jacobite songs already circulating through the country, he had little difficulty in gathering a body of men pledged to the Stuart cause; but at Sheriffmuir he was among the most faint-hearted of the fugitives. He is ranked as "even" with Seaforth and Huntly.

Almost simultaneously with the suppression

of the Rebellion in the north, the Border Rising, headed on the Scottish side by Lord Kenmure, came to a disastrous end. The first of the Jacobite Border ballads of historical note appears to be *Kenmure's on an' awa'*. As before arranged, the south Scottish Jacobites were re-inforced by a body of about two thousand Highlanders, sent to their assistance by Mar, under the guidance of the brave and daring veteran of Borlam, Brigadier Macintosh. He had boldly crossed the Firth of Forth in open boats in face of the Government fleet, had captured Leith, frightened the Whig citizens of Edinburgh, crossed the Lammermuirs to Dunse, and joined Kenmure near Kelso. The plan he proposed to the border leaders was to co-operate directly with Mar's forces in Perthshire by marching to Stirling and enclosing Argyll between two fires; but his policy was, unluckily for the Jacobite interests, over-ruled; he was induced to add his forces to the insurrectionary army of Derwentwater and Foster, then mustered on the English side of the

Border; and so shared in the misfortunes and ruin of that ill-managed campaign which terminated in the disgraceful surrender of Preston. The ballads connected with these border events are loud in the imputation of cowardice and treachery against Foster, and in their admiration of the courage and military honour of " Old Macintosh," as he is commonly styled.

After the disasters at Sheriffmuir and at Preston, and in spite of the arrival of the Chevalier, the insurgent army dispersed; and executions and imprisonments followed. The fortunes of the Stuarts were about this time at their lowest ebb. Every step in " the Fifteen " had been so badly timed that the Chevalier was fain to go back again to France and wait for another tide which should lead to fortune,—but which never again offered so favourably.

The Jacobites in Scotland, in the meantime, sought to keep alive the feeling of discontent with the House of Guelph, by lampoons on the government, and personal attacks of a satirical and calumnious nature upon the reigning family. A good deal of their energy also found vent in bitter accusations and recriminations of each other. At last their tone appeared to change, as the figure of " Prince Charlie," the young Chevalier, began to rise on the political horizon. His beauty, grace, agreeable manners, and war-like disposition heralded his coming; and when at last the news came from Moidart to over-run the country like wildfire, that the royal adven-turer was on Scottish ground, the fading hopes of the Jacobites began to brighten and broaden. Affairs were in a condition not less unfavourable to the cause than they shewed in 1716, yet the devotion and loyalty his person and circumstances inspired soon surrounded him with an army of Highlanders, with which he boldly sought the field. Never was Prince more beloved. The songs and ballads that welcomed his arrival bespeak the most ardent enthusiasm. They are all in praise of his princely behaviour, and breathe the most devoted wishes for his success.

Many of them are in the Gaelic tongue, and these, for fervour of language and unanimity of sentiment, are unmatched in any literature. They will be noticed hereafter. It is unnecessary, here, to trace minutely the events of " the Forty-five." It will be sufficient to glance at the broader features of that Rebellion. The defeat of Sir John Cope at Prestonpans, and the triumphal return to Edinburgh, raised the hopes of the Jacobites to the highest pitch. The unfortunate Cope was pitilessly tortured by the ballad-mongers of the day. Nothing of all that he had said or done in connexion with the battle of Prestonpans, was lost sight of, or unutilized, to his disadvantage. And each of the many accounts of his conduct at that battle left him at Dunbar or Berwick telling the story of his own defeat. After the victory, the forces of Charles continued to increase; and in swelling the ranks of the Jacobite army, female influence, as exerted upon husband, brother, or lover, played a significant part. At length the march to England was resolved upon. The border was crossed, and Carlisle taken. The English Jacobites, however, were slow to commit themselves to the side they secretly cherished. They wanted to be more sure of its proving the winning side. This was the general feeling among them,—so that the backwardness of each deterred his neighbour. The Jacobite army reached Derby,—but still there were no decided signs of encouragement held out by the English. The halt at Derby was the turning point of the cause. Retreat was resolved on, and the star of Jacobitism approached its setting. Dissensions divided the leaders, privations and inaction disheartened the men, and the Government was daily recovering strength and decision. A brief glimpse of victory shone on the Jacobite arms at Falkirk, where General Hawley was driven from the field. The ballads of this battle allude to the fierce wind that blew in the face of the Government army, and to the sudden and unexpected disappearance of the foe:

N

> " Says brave Lochiel, ' Pray, have we won ?
> I see no troop, I hear no gun ';
> Says Drummond, ''Faith the battle's done,
> I know not how nor why.'"

The Prince, however, was still forced to retreat. Winter was spent among the Highlands, and in the ensuing Spring the fatal blow was dealt to Jacobitism on the moor of Culloden. From this point onwards in the ballad-history of the Jacobites, hope is either entirely lost, or shines with only a transient ray. The vengeance of Heaven is invoked upon the merciless conquerors; but the prevailing strain is one of lamentation and despondency. Satire still continues, but it is no longer in any of its moods playful or hopeful: it is earnestly acrimonious, and tinged with despair. Indeed, the sorrow that befell the Jacobite party by the disaster of Culloden, gave quite a new character to the bulk of the song-literature of that and subsequent years. It increased and refined the poetry of the literature. We might even say, speaking comparatively of the ballads preceding

the year 1746, and those of that and the immediately succeeding years, that the sorrows of
the Stuarts were unconsecrated by song till fate
at last fairly determined for doom that the
House should fall. Then the recollection of
the earlier misfortunes, which, however, seemed
only partial while the struggle was going on
and fate had not yet indicated the disastrous
final result, deepened the sorrow and refined
the song.

After the battle, executions and confiscations
followed, and a price was set on the head of the
fugitive prince. The loyalty of the Highlands
kept him safe. " Though thirty thousand pounds
they gi'e, where's the knave that would betray?"
And again, in spite of all the sufferings that had
been entailed upon the Highlanders by their
active support of his cause, with unflinching
devotion they could sing,—

> " He gat the skaith, he gat the scorn,—
>   I lo'e him yet the better;
> Tho' in the muir I hide forlorn,
>   I'll drink his health in water!"

It would seem that a hope of rallying the clans after Culloden, existed among some of the fugitive Jacobites: "Prince Charlie he'll be down again," &c.; and,—

> " I yet may stand as I ha'e stood
>   Wi' him thro' rout an' slaughter,
> An' bathe my hands in scoundrel blood
>   As I do now in water!"

This hope, however,—at least its immediate fulfilment,—was soon abandoned; and the bards of the cause confined their strains to hopes of the personal safety of their wandering prince, and continued expressions of devotion to his service:

> " I'll hide thee in Clanranald's isles
>   Where honour still bears sway;
> I'll watch the traitor's hovering sails
>   By islet and by bay."

The Prince's companion and guide in his skulkings among the glens, and moors, and islands of the inner Hebrides, is frequently mentioned, and always with honour and admiration, in this connexion. And when at last his wanderings are over, and he is safely embarked, and safely landed in France, the cry of the almost heartbroken Jacobite breaks out in the refrain,— "Will ye no' come back again?" Years after he had left, his memory was cherished. He was invited back, and promised the utmost help which in their ruined condition they could bestow. They were willing to sacrifice their last drop of blood in his service, as many of them had already sacrificed the last acres of their patrimony. Mothers even promised their remaining sons in proof of the cheerfulness with which they had granted the lives of their elder-born to his cause. So late as 1772 the spirit of active Jacobitism was kept alive. In April of that year the Prince married Louisa of Stolberg and the union inspired considerable joy and fresh hopes in the breasts of the Scottish Jacobites. The lady at once became the subject of loyal toasts. But the sword had been lifted for the last time in behalf of the Stuarts in April 1746, and the once vigorous feeling of Jacobitism

began to sink into mere romantic sentimental-
ism.

Not the least interesting feature of the
Jacobite Ballads lies in the numerous incidental
references to the customs of the age, and to the
social, moral, and religious condition of the
nation. These allusions afford vivid side-
glimpses of the home-life of the people. Thus,
from the numerous toasts and healths, the large
enumeration of "horns" and glasses, which
occur in the Songs, we learn that the Jacobite
age must have been an intensely thirsty one.
Drinking appears to have been reckoned a
manly and fashionable accomplishment; and
the person who would refuse to honour a toast,
that did not shock his political ideas even, would
have been obliged to leave the company, and
held in suspicion by his bacchanalian confrères.
"Take off the toast," is the order of the feast-
master, "for he that refuses, a traitor we'll
mark." From the drinking tendencies of the
age, social gatherings were of frequent occur-

rence, where were discussed the plans of the
Stuart restoration, and the chances of success
likely to be relied on. "A running bumper" is
called for to the health of the "royal Swede."
"Then let us be jovial, social, and free," is part
of a swinging chorus. "I'se be fou, an' thou'se
be toom, cogie, an the king come," is the quaint
utterance of a resolution likely to be acted up to,
from its very undemonstrativeness. Just before
the dismissal of a company, met to concoct
schemes inimical to the government, the cry of
the host is,—

> "Send roun' the usquebaugh sae clear;
> Let's tak' a horn thegither;"

and, as a parting advice to those whose attach-
ment to Jacobitism was in danger of effervescing
in noisy professions over the alcohol, the lines
of the song are quoted,—

> "He that drinks maun fight too,
> To shew his heart's upright too."

Attendant upon these social gatherings were
the pastimes of piping and dancing. In fact a

piper was an indispensable at a Jacobite meeting. And dancing is frequently spoken of as if it were the usual concomitant of the strains of the bagpipe :

> " Mak' the piper blaw,
>   An' let the lads and lasses baith
> Their supple legs shaw ! "

is the command of a south-country "laird" to whom is brought the intelligence of the expected arrival of his exiled king.

In connexion with these cheerful recreations of the Stuart partizans, we may notice the contempt they entertained for the sunless severity and austerity of life of the Cameronians, or Scottish Puritans. They ridiculed and mocked them in many ways,—in their garb, features, talk, doctrines,—and especially in the mode of life they adopted, so destructive of the little sweets. of social companionship. The mock solemnity of the ballad of the *Cameronian Cat*, that followed its feline instincts of mouse-catching on a Sunday, is a bitter caricature of the external strictness in Sabbatarian observances of the stern Hill-men of the West. Latterly in the Jacobite struggle they were let alone for the most part. Many of them, indeed, had become so dissatisfied with the Union, and with the treatment of Scotland in commercial matters by the English, that they were secretly inclining to the Jacobite side,—a state of matters which was not long in leaking out, and of which the Chevalier was not slow to take advantage for the furtherance of his claims. In a manifesto, dated 31st October, 1718, with a view to securing their aid, or at least their non-interference in any after attempts he might make against the Hanoverian Government, he promised to "protect such of our people, commonly called Cameronians, as shall prove dutiful and loyal to us, from all sorts of hardships and oppressions." The Hill-men as a class, however, had conceived a strong—in some cases, an ineradicable dislike to the very name of Stuart, ever since the persecutions to which their fathers and themselves had been subjected in the reigns of Charles and James; and, consequently, the manifesto of the Chevalier was without result.

The occupation of spinning, &c., then common to the female portion of the lower and even middle class, is often alluded to. From Buchan, we have enthusiasm for the white cockade blending with the sentiment of love, expressed in the lines,—

> " I'll sell my rock, I'll sell my reel,
>   My ripplin' kame, an' spinnin' wheel,
>   To buy my lad a tartan plaid,
>   A broad-sword, and a white cockade."

And, again, in the spirited verses of Lady Drummond,—

> " I may sit in my wee croo' house,
>   At the rock an' the reel to toil fu' dreary," &c.

Many of the ballads have a country air about them: they smack undeniably of the farmyard and the sheepfold. "What a delightful picture," says the Ettrick Shepherd, "of our ancient and homely hospitality do these few lines convey,—

> ' Wi' rowth o' kin, an' rowth o' reek,
>   My daddy's door it wadna steek;
> But bread an' cheese were his door-cheek,
>   An' girdle-cakes the riggin' o't.' "

In the song beginning "What ails thee, puir Shepherd ? " we have Britain viewed as an extensive sheep-farm, and, from the Jacobite point of view, hastening to ruin from the unskilfulness and roguery of its "shepherds." In a song already quoted, two fugitive Jacobite lords from Sheriffmuir are spoken of as better adapted to act as shepherdesses than as soldiers. One of the ballads about the battle of Sheriffmuir begins, " O cam' ye here the fight to shun, or herd the sheep wi' me ? " In another ballad, a disguised Jacobite is represented as climbing the hillside to "shift his sheep their lair." A third has the verse, which the closing days of Walter Scott have filled with a melancholy interest,—

> " It's up yon heathery mountain,
>   An' doun yon scroggy glen,
> We daurna gang a milkin',
>   For Charlie an' his men."

The profligacy, open and unchecked, which reigned at the court, especially of the first George, was unsparingly exposed by the Jacobite satirists. This was fair game for the shafts of satire; but delicacy was required in the matter, and in this respect the Jacobite bards have been awanting. They never encourage vice, and they never deride or jest at virtue; on the contrary, they denounce vice, but in terms of wide-mouthed coarseness. Dealing with a foul subject, they are careless in their mode of treatment of it, and so contract some of the foulness to themselves. In their hatred, too, of their political opponents, the Jacobite bards frequently approach the verge of blasphemy, as well as indulge in coarseness. But this can more commonly be predicated of the language than of the idea; and, taking the literature of the period all in all as a fair reflection of the state of matters in Scotland at the time it was produced, we must acknowledge that, between that time and this, Scotland was yet to reach her greatest depth of profanity and blasphemy.

But the Jacobite ballads of Scotland may be viewed in another and totally different light from that in which we have hitherto been regarding them. They are a repository of interesting historical facts relating to the period when they first appeared; but this, for the most part, they are only incidentally: the main object of their production is not now the palpable thing it was when they were first given in successive instalments to the world. They exercised an influence,—and a mighty influence, in the cause they advocated. They are now merely the historical frame-work or skeleton of an energy that no longer lives and breathes in them. This principle of life and action,—this influence, we have seen, died hard. It was succeeded by a weaker influence of less potent range,—a watery dilution of the former, which was confined entirely to the region of imagination. It appeared only in words: otherwise it did not reach the outer world of life and action. It fought and struggled only in imagination, and exercised no governing sway over the outward life. There were thus two species of Jacobitism; the one, real, active, outward; the other, sentimental, romantic, fanciful. The latter we shall consider in its proper place, as an out-growth, or rather after-growth, of the former. And, in the meantime, let us confine ourselves shortly to the Jacobitism of the Jacobite ballads, viewed in the aspect of a principle of action.

All literatures affect the age of which they are the outcome. They are not merely mirrors in which later generations may trace the broader mental features of their predecessors. They were not simply the passive recipients of the thoughts and feelings of the age: they were active as well as passive, and helped to modify, and perhaps even create the very features which they now hold up as characteristic of the age in which they were produced. This is true of the literatures of peaceful times: much more palpably is it true when asserted of a period of struggle and controversy,—such as the period before us,—when the minds of men are over-heated, and readily and decisively moved in the direction to which they are naturally inclined.

We may consider, in the first place, the cementing influence which the ballads exercised over the scattered energies of the Jacobite party. They gave unity and individuality to Jacobitism, and thus acted as a powerful aid in perfecting the policy laid down by its leaders. A ballad which contained the plans or the hopes of the Jacobite leaders was longer-lived than the spoken word or communicated letter, penetrated into remoter localties, and gave a more extensive publicity. By this means the collective energy of the Jacobite body was prevented from being frittered away and lost in desultory and independent movements, and greater unity of action was secured when the time came to strike a blow. They also revealed to the members of the party as a collective body their own strength, and gave them a confidence in themselves which they could not otherwise have possessed. By

the free use of names they marked out in a clear
and unmistakeable manner the number and
strength of the adherents of Jacobitism. They
confirmed the wavering, the irresolute, and the
faint-hearted, while at the same time they prevented the double-dealing from tampering with
Jacobite matters. A man whose name was
sounded in the same song with well-known and
determined advocates of the Stuart cause, must
have understood that from that moment he had
taken the decisive step which separated him
from the Government, and placed him among
the ranks of the Jacobites; and from the moment
of his public committal to that party, he must
have been stimulated to the utmost to further
the advancement of the interests with which
his name was now bound up, from a sense that
his own safety depended upon the exertions of
his party. Not only therefore would the ballad-
literature increase the strength of the Jacobites,
by collecting their various and far-separated
energies into a unity, but it would still further

add to their collective strength, by inciting individual action to the highest pitch.

In yet another way would the ballads stir up the Jacobite partizans to the display of great individual exertion. When they were in the field, and a battle impending, they were not only conscious of the disasters that would be sure to befall them if they should chance to be unsuccessful as a body: they were further aware that, however the issue should go, brave and honourable behaviour on their part as individual soldiers would certainly be noted, and sung about, and circulated ere many days throughout the country; and that, on the other hand, cowardice or treachery, wherever witnessed,— and, if enacted, it could not very well wholly escape notice, — would be unsparingly proclaimed, and as loudly by friend as by foe. The ballads, in fact, in their accounts of the battles of the Jacobite Rebellion, filled the position of the modern newspaper, with this difference, that they were ten-fold more severe in their comments upon cowardice and treachery, and held up the unfortunate subjects of their satire and denunciation to a much longer-lived obloquy. At the same time, furnished as they were by rhyme with wings and talons, they were as universal in their range, and clung more continuously and forcibly to the memories of men. Thus, the additional stimulus of fame, or at least the preservation of honour, was brought to bear with peculiar force upon the adherents of Jacobitism, by the well-known character of these ballads. Cowards and traitors were lashed unmercifully by the thong of the satirist. Indeed, so bitterly was the behaviour of Huntly, Seaforth, and Carnegie of Phinaven assailed for the timidity and evil example they exhibited at Sheriffmuir, that they were afraid to show face again among their own party, and accordingly deserted to the other side. In this way, the Jacobite camp was kept pure, by the deterrent influence exercised by the ballads upon occasions of the faintest symptoms of cowardice.

But the ballads acted further as an influence in inducing individuals to throw in their lot with Jacobitism, by an enumeration of the claims the Stuarts had upon their loyalty and allegiance. These claims are sometimes expressly set forth, and altogether embrace a variety of considerations. One of the writers declares that by the laws of God the Stuarts must, and yet shall, reign ; the date of their restoration may be delayed, but the country will never rest in peace till these laws are satisfied. He even represents religion to be an impossible thing in the country while the Stuarts remain in exile. He says,—

> " To injure true princes and gloss o'er offences
> Is serving God worse than a Turk or a Jew.
> Then what we so foully have taken away,
> O let us return on our reckoning day,
> Or else we as wicked as demons are grown ;
> And tho' to the skies
> We turn up our eyes,
> Dishonour the church and the land we own."

And again, in a kindred strain,—

> " Your Hogan Mogan foreign things,
> God gave them in displeasure," &c.

Then, as visible proofs of the divine displeasure, he traces the disasters of Scotland to the establishment of these contemptuous " foreign things " in the land of the Stuarts:—

> " Our Darien can witness bear
>   And so can our Glencoe,
> Our South Sea it can make appear
>   What to your kings we owe.
> We have been murder'd, starv'd, and robb'd,
>   By those your kings and knavery;
> And all our treasure is stock-jobbed
>   While we groan under slavery."

The only possible plan of ending these calamities, and averting the mischief which they have produced,—in the words of the song,—

> " The only way relief to bring,
>   And save both church and steeple,
> Is to bring in our lawful king,
>   The father of his people.
> Ne'er can another fill his place
>   O'er rights divine and civil."

In another song, James, " the Pretender " of the whigs, is called by the Jacobite bard " your God's vicegerent and your king."

Another argument made use of to enforce the Stuart claims is the high antiquity of the family.

> " His great progenitors have sway'd
>   Your sceptre *nigh the half of time.*"

The birth of the Chevalier is even the fulfilment of a prophecy uttered ages ago, according to the Jacobite bard. " 'Twas thus," says he, reading his prophecy backwards,—

> " 'Twas thus *in early bloom of time,*
>   Under a reverend oak,
> In sacred and inspired rhyme
>   An ancient Druid spoke,—
> ' An hero from fair Clementine
>   Long ages hence shall spring,
> And all the gods their power combine
>   To bless the future king.' "

Similar arguments were largely circulated in pamphlet-form on the accession of George I. " I'm confident," says one writer, in an expostulatory address, "that in our secret thoughts we are agreed that King James VIII. is our lawful rightful sovereign; and we all know that he is the undoubted lineal heir by blood, and descendant of the ancient race of our Scottish kings, whose ancestors, in a direct line, have swayed the sceptre in our hereditary monarchy for many generations without control; a prince upon whom the crown is entailed by the fundamental laws of our country; and to whom, even before he was born, we have often sworn allegiance and fealty by those oaths given to former kings, by which we bound ourselves not only to them, but to their lawful heirs and successors, &c., &c."

The ballads lay strong force on the Stuarts being native to Scotland; and the fact of their being "foreigners" is again and again urged against William and the Georges as sufficient in itself to disqualify them from wielding the Stuart sceptre. In the spirit-stirring song *Wha wadna fecht for Charlie?* the verse occurs illustrative of this,—

> " Shall we basely crouch to tyrants,
> Shall we own a *foreign* sway;
> Shall a royal Stuart be banished,
> While a *Stranger* rules the day?"

The same idea comes out prominently in the

pamphlet-literature of the day:—"You are to fight against your lawful and rightful king, born in our own island, of the ancient stock of the royal family of the Stuarts."

Every method is adopted to recommend "Prince Charlie" to the people of Scotland. His handsome appearance, princely manners, native courtesy, and courage, are all praised again and again; and his name is linked with one which every Scotsman must always respect with complete unanimity of feeling,—the name of the Bruce. He is called the "Bruce's Heir," and therefore Scotland was his rightful patrimony:

> "The hills he trode were a' his ain; . . .
> The bush that hid him on the plain
> There's nane on earth can claim but he."

Ingratitude is charged in the pamphlets, where they treat of the same arguments, against those who are about to draw their swords against the cause of the Stuarts:—"His ancestors bravely defended us, and transmitted down to us the liberty and independency of our nation; and under them our nobility and gentry first received, and ever since possessed, all the honours, titles, riches, and estates, &c."

To meet the wishes and secure the aid of those whose only objections to "the Pretender" are his popish education and intolerant papistical creed, the pamphleteer offers the assurance that "he is truly of the one Catholic Church, without the addition of Roman." And, further, "But let the king's religion be what it will, he has under his hand given us all the security we can ask that he will maintain the Protestant Religion in his kingdoms, and fence it from any danger by such laws, as shall, by the advice of his Parliament, be thought necessary."

The influence of party-song in keeping alive the spirit of the cause, in support of which they were framed, is too manifest to require more than a passing allusion. King Edward the First of England sought to destroy this influence in the prosecution of his conquest of Wales, by compassing the death of the Welsh bards, and suppressing the patriotic strains in praise of freedom and independence, which formed the main bulwark of the land of the Cymri. It was by the universal prevalence of a single party-song that James II. was said, with considerable show of truth, to have been "whistled" and sung out of his ancestral inheritance. So fully acknowledged, indeed, has the power of song become in the formation and guidance of national opinion, that the saying, attributed to Fletcher of Saltoun, "Give me the making of a country's songs, and let who will make its laws," has passed into a proverb. It is perhaps difficult, therefore, to over-estimate the influence of the Jacobite ballads upon the prolongation of the struggle between the rival parties in Britain during the sixty years from the Revolution. In that period three important risings took place, the attempts, namely, of Dundee, Mar, and the young Chevalier respectively, to re-instate the Stuart dynasty. These attempts mark the epochs when the struggle gathered to a head, and burst out fiercely in civil war. Between these points or centres of activity stretched years of apparent repose, which, however, were prevented from sinking into apathy, indifference, or forgetfulness, by the constant circulation throughout the country of ballads breathing the most ardent devotion to Jacobitism, and the most determined opposition to what they regarded as foreign supremacy. These ballads were repeated from town to town, and from village to village; they were sung at secret social gatherings of the Jacobites; they were treasured in every Jacobite memory; and thus rendered it impossible that the principles of Jacobitism should speedily die and be forgotten. They were taught by Jacobite parents to their children as, next to the Bible, the most important part of their education, instilling into their minds the principles of loyalty, and furnishing them with a political creed by which to direct their lives and actions:

Indeed, in some of the more intensely Jacobite households, the spirit of these ballads was inculcated into the minds of the rising generation as a species of religion. The exiled heir was God's vicegerent on earth; want of loyalty to him was breach of faith with God. To the grown-up Jacobite, whose mind did not require their teaching,—coëval as it was with their earliest production,—the ballads came endowed with hardly less important influences. They cheered him in his hours of despondency, inspired him with fresh hopes for the ultimate success of the cause to which he was pledged, and encouraged him to renewed exertions in the Stuart interest when a favourable opportunity for action should arrive. At the same time they increased his hatred and aversion to the government of a sovereign whose innermost sympathies were with his Dutch or German subjects, and whose language, customs, and traditional instincts, were comparatively alien to the British nation.

When Jacobitism as a principle of action was dead, there appeared in the country a post-humous Jacobitism of a purely sentimental type. Its sway was wholly in the realms of a romantic imagination. It gave a peculiar complexion to the literature of Scotland when, after the turmoil of the rebellions had ceased, the current of the national literature resumed its interrupted course; but beyond the pale of literature it did not reach. It was purely literary in its aim, and was quite unmixed with politics. The romantic circumstances in which real Jacobitism was fought out, the heroism, chivalry, unselfish devotion, and unparalleled misfortunes of the Stuart family and its adherents, viewed historically, contained many of the elements of poetry, and possessed strong affinity for the poetical mind. Perhaps poetical feeling was most strongly roused to the side of Jacobitism by the misfortunes which befel the ancient House of Stuart in the person of its last youthful representative, Prince Charles. This feeling was, at least, purely poetical, and would have been as readily awakened if similar circumstances had surrounded the ruin of a different family. The losing side is always the side on which the greatest amount of good poetry is enlisted. A sense of poetical justice, demanding to be shewn to the undeserving sufferers, arises in the poetical mind; and while Fate has crowned the conquering side with laurel, Poetry weaves for the prostrate vanquished a chaplet of more undying bay.

The posthumous influence of Jacobitism shewed itself, in the first place, in a continuation of the mournful strain which broke out in the ballads with such thrilling pathos after Culloden. Jacobitism, as a living principle of action, was now dead. It was hopeless to expect its resurrection. It was now only a feeling. And in this new light of it, it was gazed backwards upon in its entirety. The changes it had undergone were reviewed. The sufferings it had experienced were lingered over. The good qualities that had marked its existence were enumerated, treasured up,—in many cases, a fictitious value put upon them. Everything that could excite sympathy for the fallen family was eagerly sought out by the poetical mind, eagerly caught hold of, and lovingly shewn off in song and ballad. The sufferings and misfortunes of the Jacobite leaders,—and especially of the Prince, the most conspicuous in his sorrows of them all— were mostly dwelt upon in these songs. Many of them, by nameless bards, are fraught with the most touching pathos. They appear to have been flung off, in many cases anonymously, as a natural and only mode of relief to the sorrow-o'erburdened mind, and not from ulterior ends of poetical renown.

But to leave these scattered, and, in many cases, unacknowledged songs, and to confine our attention to the works of well-known Scottish authors whose minds have been tinged with the feeling of Jacobitism, we may notice unmistakeable traces of Jacobite predilection in the poetry of Carolina Oliphant, Baroness Nairne, of Burns, of Hogg, of Scott, and, not to exhaust the whole list, of Campbell, and of Aytoun. Some of the best so-called Jacobite songs are by Lady Nairne. And, possessing as she did in a marked degree the genius of the lyre, it would have been matter of surprise if she had turned away her attention from the misfortunes of the House of Stuart. Her father, her grandfather, and numerous relatives, were among the most zealous and active supporters of Jacobitism in the period of the rebellions. She was born and educated in "the Auld House of Gask,"— which was a very centre of Jacobite ideas. She was taught to sing the praises of the Stuarts ere she could well lisp the name. Her family had shared in the misfortunes of the exiled family. And many little acts of special favour had been extended to her father by the young Chevalier himself. Accordingly, her songs are imbued with the spirit of Jacobitism, and are so clearly the offspring of the heart, that none are more widely known or more universally popular among Scotsmen. So completely is the feeling of Jacobitism mixed up in her mind with all other feelings, that it shews itself even in songs that have no direct connexion with Jacobitism. One of the many associations, for instance, by which "the Auld House" of her childhood,—in the deservedly popular song of that name,—has become endeared to her memory, is the circumstance that the eyes of "Scotland's Heir" have rested upon its walls; and that it contains, as one of its most cherished treasures, a lock of "his lang yellow hair."

Burns, it is well known, was strongly touched with the misfortunes that at last overwhelmed the Stuart line. This sympathetic feeling occasionally bursts out in his songs, though he evidently laboured to restrain it. He even apologises to those who might take his strongly-uttered expressions of sympathy for the unfor-

tunate Stuarts in other than a poetical signification:

> " A poor friendless wanderer may well claim a sigh,
> Still more if that wanderer be royal."

In the *Chevalier's Lament* occurs the well-
known line,—

> " His right are these hills, and his right are these valleys,"—

but the statement is urged simply to explain
the poetical sympathy with which his heart was
charged for one, now dead, who was chased
from his paternal inheritance. From Burns's
muse we have also *Strathallan's Lament.*

Hogg's Jacobite predilections in literature
were even more marked, but not more decidedly
intense than Burns's. He has got his comic
as well as his plaintive Jacobite songs. Of the
former class, perhaps the most original is
Donald Macgillivray. It is amusing to find
"the Shepherd" at one time giving it as his
opinion "that *Donald Macgillivray* is apparently
a very old song, and doubtless is meant to
embrace the whole Highland clans under an

P

individual name"; and, at another time, as a great secret, avowing himself the author of it. A verse of it runs thus,—descriptive of the fierce descent of the Highlanders upon the Lowlands in aid of the Stuart cause,—

" Donald's run ower the hill, bot his tether, man,
 As he were wud, or stang'd wi' an ether, man;
 When he comes back, there's some will look merrily;
 Here's to King James, and Donald Macgillivray.
 Come like a weaver, Donald Macgillivray,
 Come like a weaver, Donald Macgillivray,
 Pack on your back, an' elwan' sae cleverly;
 Gie them full measure, my Donald Macgillivray!"

But Hogg's genius as a Jacobite song-writer is best manifested in those translations from the Gaelic illustrative of Celtic hospitality and loyalty to the royal adventurer. *Maclean's Welcome* and *Flora Macdonald's Lament* may stand as instances.

Scott's leanings to the side of Jacobitism are visible in his *Waverley*, and in several minor songs,—chief among these the spirited *Gathering of the Clans*,—which reveal the interest he felt in the fortunes of the Stuart House. From the natural disposition of his mind, it might have been predicted of Scott that these fortunes would claim his sympathies. The passing away of a dynasty of high antiquity must have powerfully affected the mind of him to whom every time-honoured institution was sacred. Even the destruction of an old bridge called up sad and contemplative ideas in his mind. It is well known he was fond of repeating the old Jacobite ballads, and nothing gave him more pleasure, deep and undemonstrative, than to listen to the singing of those of them that bewail the sad fate of the royal wanderer. But, after all, we are less able to lay our finger upon any particular passage of Scott's works indicative of undoubted Jacobite sympathies, than to feel, in the perusal of these works as a whole, a pervading air faintly tinged with the aroma of Jacobitism.

Campbell's noble fragment of *Lochiel's Warning* sufficiently indicates the fascination with which his mind was drawn to the contemplation of the tragic downfall of the Stuart House,—a downfall that included in its completeness the ruin of so many devoted partizans. His feelings, too, as shewn in the single brief fragment, are all on the losing side.

But of all the modern Scottish authors whose works shew a Jacobite leaning, none perhaps has been more thoroughly steeped in Jacobitism than Aytoun. With him, Jacobitism was a passion; and so effectually colours the whole body of his poetry, that one might say his genius only lived, and was only inspired, to celebrate in immortal verse the later fortunes of the Stuarts. Sympathies of a warmer or more absorbing character in behalf of Jacobitism, are nowhere to be found in the entire collection of literature born of the Stuart struggle after a restoration. So intense, indeed, were these sympathies, that they have warped his whole mental energies, and confined them to the single task of setting forth the strangely-mingled glories and reverses of the loyal Scottish Cavaliers. And this is the great fault of his poetry: it is too narrow, too exclusive and one-sided. His hatred of the enemies of the Stuarts is unjustly severe and intolerant. He can see nothing in them to admire, or even respect. They were all hypocrites, traitors, or cowards; just as all his cavaliers were heroes, loyal subjects, and men of truth.

There is still prevalent in the country an influence possessed by the Jacobite songs which can most aptly be described as traditional. This influence is, no doubt, greatly due to the intrinsic literary merits of many of the songs; but is chiefly owing to early association. Let us again recollect that they were once the only songs in the mouth of an entire generation: they were sung everywhere,—crooned as cradle-songs, adapted as love-songs, and sung as impassioned expressions of freedom and patriotism. They were thus intimately interwoven with the every-day life of our forefathers. To the old and the middle-aged, they were fraught with associations of times, persons, and places in the past, whither the memory loved to turn;—at the same time they were flung in the way of the young, by whom they were seized, and used as the fittest expressions of their own individual experiences and modes of thought and feeling. In this way, they have come down to our own generation with almost unimpaired popularity,—despite of many excellent rival songs,—but, of course, with greatly altered signification. Their present influence is eminently healthful. Songs that bring back to one's recollection childhood, parents, and the disinterested friendships of early youth, cannot but tend to keep the mind fresh, and pure, and true to its youthful instincts. This influence they exercise as derived from associative sources. To this, add the further beneficial influence springing from intrinsic virtues of courage, fidelity, and patriotism, which they inculcate in homely but frequently fervid phrase.

It now remains for us to take a survey of the

songs and ballads, born of Jacobitism, with a
view to a judgment of their literary value, and
a determination of their prevailing characteristics. Produced, as by far the greater proportion of them were, in a controversial age, when
party spirit ran high, we are not surprised to
find that many of them are of a satirical nature.
Much of this satire is only rhymed abuse,—
quite devoid of any poetical thought or feeling.
The object of the satire appears to have been
thought attained, if the person at whom its
shafts were launched was seen to wince under
the infliction. A good deal of it is coarse;
rather, however, in expression than in idea.
This was natural, when we consider the heated
passions of the times. Men, in their angry
haste, said things which in their calmer moods
they would have been shocked to hear. They
attacked each other's character with the imputation of the foulest, and often only fanciful,
crimes. They swore dreadful oaths of hatred
and vengeance against each other, and reck-

lessly condemned each other's soul to ever-lasting torment. What wonder if, occasionally, such coarseness, and curses so dreadful, found their way into the satirical literature of the day? But there still remains, after deducting these, a considerable amount of good and legitimate satire. A peculiar feature of this satire is the microscopical insignificance to which it dwarfs what it regards as ambitious pretension. As an example of this, take the ballad of the *Wee wee German Lairdie*. The very name with which they speak of King George is satirical in the highest degree. He is spoken of as having been elevated to a position which he never even aspired to:

> "When we gade to bring him hame,
>   He was delvin' in his kail-yardie."

He is represented as bringing in his train a number of indigent dependents, who are briefly discussed as "fouth o' foreign trash." His presence on the throne of England, however, is nothing to the Scottish satirist,—only let him stay there. If ever he crosses the Tweed to the ancient kingdom of Scotland, it must in no case be with the pretentions of a sovereign. That could not for a moment be tolerated. These assumed pretensions must then be laid aside. He must in nowise presume to intermeddle with the time-hallowed institutions of Scotland. He is invited to visit and admire, or sink abashed,— but not to touch, overturn, or revolutionize.

> " Come up among our highland hills,
>   Thou wee wee German Lairdie,
> An' see how the Stuarts' lang-kail thrive
>   They dibbled in our yardie !
> An' if a stock ye daur to pu',
> Or haud the yokin' o' a plou',
> We'll break your sceptre owre your mou',
>   Thou wee bit German Lairdie !"

More frequently, however, the satire of these ballads is, metaphorically speaking, a furious succession of knock-down blows, distributed with little discrimination, and less mercy. The only object is to pommel into shapelessness. The fine art to which Pope ennobled the science of literary abuse was unknown, or at least unappreciated in Scotland. The Scottish satirists did not waste their time and expend their fury in polishing and pointing their instrument of attack. They were too hot-blooded for that. Nor did they take delicate aim from behind some loophole in front of which the enemy was thoughtlessly breathing himself, with armour laid aside or vizor up. The object of their attack had notice, for the most part, of the intended assault; the bolts, sharp or blunt, as they came to hand, were shot off at random, and when they were exhausted the butt of the cross-bow was a handy instrument of offence. Thus Scottish satire rather bestowed surface bruises, which stunned as much by the noise as the pain with which their delivery was accompanied,—than poisoned wounds that rankled secretly, and bled inwardly, and were long and painful in healing. This had from time immemorial been the orthodox mode of dealing literary castigation in Scotland. Dunbar was an adept in it, and Lyndsay and all the literary disciplinarians of the past had so taught the art. To illustrate this mode of satirical writing, so often adopted by the contributors to the Jacobite ballad-literature, look for a moment on this wholesale onslaught upon the *Whigs of Fife:*—

> " O, for a bauk as lang as Crail,
>   An' for a rape o' rapes the wale,
>   To hing the tykes up by the tail
>   An' hear the beggars yell!
>
> O, wae to a' the Whigs o' Fife,
> The brosy tykes, the lousy tykes,
> O, wae to a' the Whigs o' Fife
>   That e'er they cam' frae," &c.

One can fancy the Whigs of Fife themselves, after this tremendous deluge of wordy invective, recovering their scattered ideas, and laughing immoderately at the imaginary gallows of Herculean dimensions, with its abnormally-strung load of yelping curs. In the same song the writer prays for the return of that happy day when "ilka ane shall get his ain, an' ilka Whig the *mell:*" he implores also that Satan be loosed among the Fife Whigs for a while "to claw the traitors wi' a *flail*." These ponderous implements of industrial occupation are fitting emblems of the author's own powers as a satirist. They break bones, and bruise, and make noise enow; but, after all, they are not the most lethal weapons which one might carry with him to the battle-field. There is often a ludicrous weirdness of imagination portrayed in this species of Jacobite Satire. Thus in the lines,—

> "O, to see Auld Nick gaun hame
> Wi' Charlie's faes afore him!"—

we have a vivid vision that half shocks us with its daring, and half shakes us into laughter with its ludicrousness.

It may be as well here to notice the frequency with which the figure of Satan is made to appear and re-appear in the long series of the Jacobite ballads. It seems, indeed, that about this time was formed that idea of the "Deil" and his supposed usual place of abode, which was afterwards more fully elaborated by the genius of Burns, and is now come to be regarded as peculiarly Scottish. Whatever may have been the origin of the Scottish idea of hell and the Devil, it was certainly not English nor German. The hell of *Paradise Lost* is a vast unexplored region of "doleful shades" through which we have sublimely indistinct glimpses of a tall, battle-scarred, archangelic figure stalking with uncomplaining pain "over the burning marle," grasping in his hand the defiant spear, and grandly terrific in his blasphemies and challenges against a greater than himself. In *Faust* he is a mixture of the sceptical philosopher and the man about town,—well versed in all the fashionable vices of a refined but licentious age, and ready with his sophistical arguments to shew that vice loses all its evil by losing all its grossness. In Scotland, on the other hand, he is represented by the Jacobite ballads as having dispensed with disguise, and as journeying about in his native nigritude. He is, however, more frequently in his own proper domain superintending the disposal of multitudinous arrivals. Rarely is he in the intermediate region of earth surveying his prospects and calculating the chances of a plenteous harvest. Occasionally, however, he is out for an airing. At one time we have him perched on the commanding site of Stirling steeple,—at another time in secret conclave with the Whig leaders; but most commonly he is immersed in the cares and anxieties of subterranean business. His occupation, as obtained from passing glimpses in the ballads, is to keep alive the fires of huge furnaces, to provide fuel, manufacture brimstone, secure the more refractory of his prisoners by gyves and chains, administer the proper rotation of punishment suited to individual cases, and, generally, preserve an ill-acknowledged supremacy. These cares he seeks to alleviate by blasphemous songs, and "scraps of Auld Calvin's catches." In that weird and powerfully imaginative poem, entitled *Cumberland and Murray's Descent*, we have a comprehensive insight into the whole infernal economy. The poem is an attack upon the cruelties perpetrated upon the defenceless Scots after Culloden by the Duke of Cumberland; and the traitorous conduct of Murray of Broughton, who, after his capture, consequent upon the suppression of "the Forty-five," was carried to London, and purchased his indemnity by discovering the secrets of many noble families concerned in the late rebellion. The Jacobite idea of justice can only be satisfied by figuring the heinousness of the crimes of these two arch-enemies to the interests of the Stuarts, as demanding all the penal resources of the place of torment. The curtain of hell is drawn aside, and an extensive underground vault of fire, smoke, brimstone, terrific noises, writhing victims, and rejoicing devils is revealed. The floor of this vault is covered with a vast sea of simmering vats, which fade away in endless series in smoky perspective. In these vats Satanic imps are now and again descried, swimming and diving, and generally disporting themselves among the mysterious contents, after the fashion of dab-chicks. At suitable distances there are great "dubs," or "lowing haughs" of fire, being constantly fed with sulphureous fuel. Around and in the midst of these are the "puir wretches" undergoing their measured allotment of punishment; while at intervals, through the flame-streaked smoke,—

> " The worm of hell, which never dies,
>   In wintled coil, writhes up an' fries! "

Each inferior demon has his own apportioned work.

> " Ae deil sat splitting brunstane matches,
>   Ane roasting Whigs like bakers' batches;
>   Ane wi' fat a Whig was bastin',
>   Spent wi' frequent pray'r an' fastin'."

Around lie the various instruments of their profession,—the hideous paraphernalia of hell: "frything pans," "caudrons," "spunks," "chains," "leisters," "scalping-whittles," and "whunstane hones." In the midst of this busy scene, the two unfortunates, in condemnation of whom the poem was written, are seized upon and submitted to the severest torments of Satanic ingenuity. Their uttered agonies are represented as unspeakable, and striking even the hardened aborigines of the region with astonishment:—

> " A' ceased when thae twin butchers roar'd,
>   An' Hell's grim Hangman stopt an' glow'r'd!"

This idea is Dantesque in its horror. Murray's greed of gain, the supposed ruling passion of his life, and his impudent cleverness in acquiring it, are represented as still accompanying him in the midst of these awful scenes:—

> " Ae deevil roar'd, till hearse an' roupit,
>   'He's pykin' the gowd frae Satan's poopit!'
>   Anither roar'd wi' eldritch yell,
>   'He's howkin the keystane oot o' hell
>   To damn us mair wi' God's day-light!'
>   An' he dookit i' the caudrons oot o' sight!
>
>   He stole auld Satan's brunstane leister,
>   Till his waukit loofs were in a blister;
>   He stole his whig-spunks, tipt wi' brunstane,
>   He stole his scalpin-whittle's whunstane;
>   An' oot o' its red-het kist he stole
>   The very charter-rights of hell !
>
>   Satan, tent weel the pilferin' villain;
>   He'll scrimp your reverence by stealin';

Q

Th' infernal boots in which you stand in,
Wi' which your worship tramps the damn'd in,—
He'll wile them aff your cloven cloots,
An' wade thro' hell-fire in your boots!"

The preparation of an infernal banquet is descibed, but with such shocking particularity of details that we cannot venture upon the subject. The "black mastiff," that guarded "the hallan gate," in the bustle of the carnival, "slipt her collar;" and, the portals being thus left unguarded, we are told, with an allusion that may perhaps determine the local origin of the poem,—

"Whigs poured in, like *Nith* in spate."

With the notice of this wholesale inundation, the poet abruptly closes his vision of hell, leaving, in another horrible but masterly tableau,—

"Hell's grim Sultan, red-wud glowrin',
Dreadin' that Whigs would usurp owre him."

This poem, as a whole, is the most original in idea, and certainly the most daring in execution in the whole compass of Jacobite literature. Indeed, it is one of the most original of all Scottish literary attempts, not even excepting

Burns's *Address to the Deil*, or his vision of unhallowed pastimes in "Alloway's Auld Haunted Kirk," in the poem of *Tam o' Shanter*. And, as regards its mode of dealing with the element of horror, we shall search any literature in vain for a poem that will over-match it.

The most apparent characteristic of the poems of the Jacobite literature as a whole, is a grim humour. Wit, in word or phrase, there is none. There is perhaps only a single attempt at wit in the collected Jacobite relics, and that is a failure. It is that species of wit usually described as the pun which the writer is attempting when he says,—

> "Sin' our true king abroad is gone
> There's nought but *Whelps* sit on his throne."

As we have already observed, the satire is for the most part humorous, and there is even a humour of the grimmest sort blending with the horrible in that most powerful and merciless of all the Satires,—*Cumberland and Murray's Descent*. But humour is distinctive of only one

side of the Scottish national mind,—the other
and equally characteristic side of which is a
most affecting pathos. There must, therefore,
be some explanation of the apparent prepon-
derance of humour in the Jacobite ballads and
songs. And this is to be sought, doubtless, in
the circumstance that the Jacobite cause remained a hopeful one down to the date of its
final extinction,—which was generally believed
by the Jacobites as a party to have happened
in or about 1746. So long as the struggle for
the Stuart restoration went on, and hope cheered
the Jacobite partizans, just so long was satirical
humour the prevailing characteristic of the contemporaneous literature. But as soon as the
clouds of fate began to collect with unmistakeable denseness over the Stuart House, and the
beams of hope to be unable to pierce these
clouds, then the tone of the literature was
changed: elegy and lament took the place of
satire and song, and a pathetic tenderness
marked the succeeding literature. A verse-

monger can write satire, but real sorrow can only be expressed melodiously by a true poetical mind. As a consequence, we find that much real poetry attended the downfall of the Stuart House, greatly superior to what accompanied the struggle when the downfall was as yet unforeseen. This has, in the histories of all individuals, families, and nations, been invariably the case. Sorrows and misfortunes are more frequently sung than joys and successes. The deeper chords of the heart, those which thrill most powerfully through a man's being, are sacred to the touch of sorrow. Hence Bannockburn as a victory is less embalmed in song than Flodden as a defeat. And Culloden as a victory is altogether unsung.

Of the pathetic Jacobite ballads and poems which appeared when the ultimate event of the struggle, though yet unforeseen, began to be whispered about forebodingly, many are in the Gaelic language. Several of these have been collected and translated, and shew the most intense devotion to the Stuarts, and the deepest sympathy for their reverses. As examples of songs illustrative of this devoted feeling, take *Lenachan's Farewell;* the *Highlander's Farewell,* in which, amidst the enumeration of his individual misfortunes, the poet is not forgetful of his prince,—

> " And thou, my prince, my injured prince,
>   Thy people have disown'd thee,
> Have hunted and have driven thee hence,
>   With ruin'd chiefs around thee.
> Though hard beset, when I forget
>   Thy fate, young helpless rover,
> This broken heart shall cease to beat
>   And all its griefs be over;"

the *Highland Widow's Lament; the Welcome to Skye; the Frasers in the Corrie; Farewell to Glen-Shalloch; Callum o' Glen; Culloden Day, &c.*

Of pathetic songs in the Lowland language, there are many examples. The mutilated fragment of *Carlisle Yetts* has a good deal of the fascinating simplicity of lament of the still older ballads of Scotland. It is a maiden's wail, and recalls to one's mind the affecting rhymes of the crazed Ophelia:—

> " His lang lang hair, in yellow hanks,
>   Waved o'er his cheeks sae sweet and ruddie;
> But now they wave o'er Carlisle yetts,
>   In dripping ringlets clotting bloodie.
>
> My father's blood's in that flower-tap,
>   My brother's in that harebell's blossom;
> This white rose was steeped in my luve's blood,
>   An' I'll aye wear it in my bosom."

The sad fate of Prince Charlie has changed the whole face of Nature to the bewailing bard. Life has now nothing joyful to offer. The once glad songs of the wild birds seem now to be turned into sorrowful refrains:

> "Whene'er I hear the blackbird sing
>   Unto the e'ening sinking doun,
> Or merle that makes the woods to ring,
>   To me they ha'e nae ither soun'
>   Than 'Will he no come back again?'" &c.

The " o'ercome," in another minstrel's ears, is " Wae's me for Prince Charlie." Even Smollett, among London distractions and London apathy, like a true son of Scotland, lets fall a few "melodious tears" in sympathetic remembrance of the misfortunes of his country.

The heroic ardour and patriotic spirit breathed by the Jacobite songs is another remarkable feature. Never was a more martial strain than the song of *Wha wadna fecht?* It contains every warlike inducement that can prompt heroic thoughts and actions. The past glories of Scottish war are recalled to mind; a prince is their leader; they are surrounded with the inspiring insignia of battle, "the pomp and circumstance of glorious war;" their numbers are increasing; the clans are advancing to swell their host with heroes; swords are flashing, pibrochs sounding—and the ancient banner of Scotland, floating over them on the buoyant winds, has to be defended.

> " Wha' wadna fecht for Charlie,
>   Wha' wadna draw the sword?"

Surely none but cowards!

Many other Jacobite ballads breathe the same

sentiments; of which we may particularly notice *Macdonald's Gathering*, and *Kenmure's on and awa'*. In the ballad of the *Lament of Lord Maxwell*, the warlike minstrel speaks of the glory of dying on the battlefield, and taking "a bluidy nievefu' o' fame to the grave."

A peculiar feature of the earlier half of the Jacobite ballads is the enigmatical and allegorical form into which many of them are cast. This appears originally to have been occasioned by the strict watch maintained by government over seditious and suspicious publications. The Jacobite rhymster accordingly took refuge under the shield of ambiguity of language, and so could sing the (in many instances) meaningless words with a mental interpretation of his own, even in public gatherings of a mixed or doubtful nature. Songs expressly Jacobite were openly sung at meetings where every member was an avowed friend of the Stuart cause; but it was necessary also to have songs that, without betraying any decided leaning this way or that, should yet act as "feelers" to test the character or political opinion of a mixed assembly. Among these enigmatical productions a good many are, naturally enough, toasts. One of them goes thus,—

> " To the turners out of the turners out
> And a return to the turnëd out,"—

and so on in such intricate fashion that the labyrinth of turnings gets quite bewildering. Another of these has much the look of a genealogical puzzle;—

> " To ane king, and no king, ane uncle and faither,
> To him that's all these, yet allowed to be neither," &c.

The Jacobite cause is symbolized in one ballad as a moor-hen, as a blackbird in another, and in a third as a cuckoo.

Sometimes the Jacobite songs admit of an interpretation of a purely amatory nature; and, of course, as such, were beyond the power of the law to suppress them. A good example of this is found in the well-known song of *Somebody*, beginning,—

"My heart is sair, I daurna tell,
My heart is sair for somebody;"

which may either be explained as the passionate
sigh of an ardent lover, wearying for the return
of his or her absent and secret sweetheart;—or,
as the longing desire of the not less ardent
Jacobite, wearying for the restoration of his
exiled king.

Allegorical songs are also of common occur-
rence among the literary products of Jacobitism.
It was noticed that allegory is often mixed up
with the Jacobite satire. George I. is a German
"Lairdie;" the kingdom is a "Kailyard;" its
institutions are "lang kail," "syboes," "leeks."
In offering counsel to Queen Anne, a Jacobite
writer represents his native country of Scotland
as "a gude gray mare," somewhat "thrawart,"
but if well-treated a useful and valuable and
obedient animal. He goes on to particularize
the successive acts of ill-treatment which had
rendered the "gray mare" unmanageable, and
worse than useless to its new owner; and advises

the adoption of judicious usage, to avoid the risk of losing it altogether. Among other songs of this nature may be enumerated *Aikendrum; The Riding Mare; There was a man came from the Moon; What ails thee, Poor Shepherd? Kirn-Milk Geordie, &c.* The allegory is sometimes so obscure as to baffle interpretation.

Glasgow Saint Andrew Society,

Instituted 30th November, 1854.

LIST OF MEMBERS
At 30th November, 1873.

OFFICE-BEARERS.

President.
G. FYFFE CHRISTIE, 62 George Square.

Vice-President.
T. MUIR GRANT, 114 West George Street.

Directors.

ALEX. WATT, *ex-officio.*	JOHN LORIMER.
FRANC GIBB DOUGALL, *ex-officio.*	JOHN WHITE.
	DANIEL MUNRO.
WILLIAM STEVENSON.	W. FORREST SALMON.

Honorary Secretary.
JOHN WIGHT, 150 Hope Street.

HONORARY MEMBERS.

ANDERSON, JAMES, Q. C., - - - -	London.
BALLANTINE, JAMES, - - - - -	Edinburgh.
BLACKIE, J. S., Professor of Greek, - -	Edinburgh.
BLIND, KARL, - - - - - -	London.
BURTON, J. H., L L. D., - - - -	Edinburgh.
BLANC, LOUIS, - - - - - -	Paris.
FREILIEGRATH, FERDINAND, - - -	Stuttgart.
FROUDE, JAMES ANTHONY, - - -	London.
GARIBALDI, GENERAL, - - - -	Caprera.
MICHEL, FRANCISQUE, - - - -	Paris.
SCOTT, CHARLES, Advocate, - - -	Edinburgh.

ORDINARY MEMBERS.

Those marked * are ex-Presidents.

Alexander, William, Jeweller, 3 Gordon Street.
Allan, P. G., 123 Argyle Street.
Allan, William, Merchant, 27 Smith Street, Whiteinch.
Arthur, John, Jeweller, 80 Argyle Street.
*Arthur, William Rae, 29 West George Street.
Auld, R. R., Writer, 49 West Regent Street.
Bain, James, 3 Park Terrace.
Baker, Thomas, Beech Bank, Mount Vernon.
Bannerman, W., Valuator, 85½ Hope Street.
Barrow, F. A., Drysalter, 191 Hope Street.
Belch, John, Merchant, 184 North Street.
Bell, B. Barton, 17 Gordon Street.
Black, George, Writer, 88 West Regent Street.
Breen, George, 18 George Square.
Bremner, George W. M., 19 St. Vincent Place.
Brownlie, John, 522 Gallowgate.
Bryan, F. G. D., Factor, Drumpellier.
Brydon, William J., 18 George Square.
Buchanan, T. D., M.D., 275 Argyle Street.
Burns, John, Surgeon, 10 John Street, Bridgeton.
Burns, Thomas, Belmont, Dowanhill.
*Burns, William, Writer, 151 St. Vincent Street.
Butler, Dugald, 12 Newhall Terrace.
Campbell, William, New Club.
Campbell, William F. M., New Club.
Carrick, John, City Master of Works, 4 South Albion Place.
Carruthers, Henry S., Writer, 150 Hope Street.
Christie, Archibald, Merchant, 87 Wilson Street.
Christie, G. Fyffe, Writer, 62 George Square, *President.*
Christie, Robert, 17 Royal Crescent, Crosshill.
Colquhoun, Alexander, 3 Ashton Place, Dowanhill.
Copland, William R., C.E., 83 West Regent Street.
Cowan, James, Brassfounder, 11 Hyde Park Street.

Craig, Bailie, 16 Abbotsford Place.
Crombie, Archibald, 5 Buchanan Street.
Cruickshank, James, Builder, 67 Bothwell Street.
Dewar, Peter, 26 Minerva Street.
Dickie, Alexander, at M. M'Farlane & Coy.'s, Distillers, Port-Dundas.
Douie, Robert, Writer, 145 Ingram Street.
*Dougall, Franc Gibb, Bank Agent, 167 Canning Street.
*Dreghorn Colonel, 5 Dixon Street.
Dunn, Hugh, Writer, 59 St. Vincent Street.
Dunn, John, High Kennedies, Hamilton.
Dykes, John, Jun., Accountant, 79 St. Vincent Street.
Ewing, George E., Sculptor, 225 Hope Street.
Faulds, W. B., Writer, 97 West George Street.
Fisher, George D., Manufacturer, 55 Wilson Street.
Fleming, James, 257 West George Street.
Forbes, John, Wine Merchant, 175 Sauchiehall Street.
Frame, Robert, Writer, Sheriff Chambers, Wilson Street.
Frame, William, Wine Merchant, 1 Ashton Place, Dowanhill.
Fraser, William, Wine Merchant, 10 Clyde Place.
Fyfe, John T., Resident Secretary, Scottish Provincial Assurance Co., 106 St. Vincent Street.
Gale, James M., Civil Engineer, 23 Miller Street.
Gardner, John, 1 Brighton Place, Govan.
Gartshore, Joseph, Falkirk.
Gemmell, Andrew, Jun., Writer, 18 Renfield Street.
Gibson, Hugh, Resident Secretary, Scottish Equitable Life Assurance Society, 128 St. Vincent Street.
Gildard, Thomas, 31 Elderslie Street.
Gillies, W. D., Metal Broker, 10 Prince's Square.
Gilmour, Graham, Merchant, 160 Buchanan Street.
Graham, John, City of Glasgow Bank, Trongate.
Grant, Donald, Manufacturer, Coatbridge.
Grant, T. Muir, Resident Secretary, Scottish Widows Fund, 114 West George Street, *Vice-President.*
Gray, David, Writer, 108 West Regent Street.

Hedderwick, James, "Citizen" Office, 34 St. Enoch Square.
Hewat, Archibald, Secretary, The Edinburgh Life Assurance
  Co., 112 St. Vincent Street.
Hinshelwood, John, St. Vincent Park, Paisley Road, Govan.
Hislop, J. B., F.R.C.S.E., 10 South Portland Street.
Hogg, William, Merchant, 81 Eglinton Street.
Hunter, Matthew, Muslin Manufacturer, 70 Union Street.
Hutcheson, Thomas S., Bookseller, 135 Buchanan Street.
Jamieson, T. B., Windham's Club, St. James Square, London.
Kay, James Cairns, 229 St. George's Road.
Kay, John Z., 229 St. George's Road.
Kaye, Robert, at R. S. Muir & Coy.'s, 46 Ingram Street.
Keir, Provost, Falkirk.
Kennedy, A., Wholesale Stationer, 13 Glassford Street.
Lamont, James, National Bank of Scotland, 174 Trongate.
Lamont, John, Merchant, 33 Virginia Street.
Lauder, Mungo, 1 Somerset Place.
Lawrence, William, 29 Kent Street.
*Leggatt, Rev. William, Buchanan Institution, 71 Greenhead
  Street.
Lindsay, George, Merchant, 34 Bedford Street.
Lockhart, James, Writer, 58 West Regent Street.
Lorimer, John, Merchant, 56 Howard Street.
Lucas, William, Writer, 133 West George Street.
M'Adam, John, 45 Hyde Park Street.
M'Call, Alexander, Chief Constable, Police Chambers.
M'Caul, James S., Merchant, 72 Ingram Street.
M'Culloch, John, Governor, Govan Poorhouse, Merryflats,
  Govan.
MacDonald, J. K., Resident Secretary, Scottish National
  Insurance Co., 120 St. Vincent Street.
M'Ewan, George, Surgeon, 196 Pitt Street.
M'Glashan, John, Merchant, 145 Stobcross Street.
M'Gregor, P. Comyn, Lonend House, Paisley.
M'Intosh, Major, 129 Stockwell Street.
Mackay, Alexander, Merchant, 212 North Street.

M'Kenzie, John, Merchant, 159 Stobcross Street.
M'Kinnon, Charles, Merchant, 1 Holland Place.
M'Kinnon, William, C. A., 140 St. Vincent Street.
M'Lachlan, Henry, Accountant, Coatbridge.
M'Onie, William, Engineer, 1 Scotland Street.
*M'Tear, Robert, Auctioneer, North Court, Royal Exchange.
Marr, Thomas, 35 St. Vincent Place.
Marshall, William, of Newhouse, Falkirk.
Mathieson, George, Warehouseman, 42 Glassford Street.
Mathieson, Thomas A., 13 East Campbell Street.
Maxton, John, Writer, 175 St. Vincent Street.
Meikleham, Lieut. William, 72 Cathedral Street.
Menzies, Thomas, F. E. I. S., Hutcheson's Hospital School,
    211 Crown Street.
Michel, Roland, Paris.
Miller, D. S., 9 Prince's Square.
Miller, Peter, 9 Prince's Square.
Mitchell, Moncrieff, C. A., 4 National Bank Buildings.
Moir, Alexander, Muslin Manufacturer, 73 Mitchell Street.
Morrison, Bailie, 52 Sauchiehall Street.
Morrison, James, Writer, 115 St. Vincent Street.
Mossman, John, Sculptor, 83 North Frederick Street.
Moyes, J. R., Stationer, 331 Sauchiehall Street.
Moyes, William, Merchant, 56 Howard Street.
Muir, Robert, 37 West Nile Street.
Munro, Daniel, 39 Hope Street.
Munro, Donald, F. C. S, Glasgow University.
'Murdoch, James, Baker, 247 Argyle Street.
Murray, D. A. B., 2 Clarendon Place.
Murray, Provost, Paisley.
Orr, William, Painter, 173 St. Vincent Street.
Park, Gavin, Measurer, 167 St. Vincent Street.
Paterson, Alexander, (of Charles M'Donald & Co.), 68
    Ingram Street.
Paton, David C., 17 Newhall Terrace.
Pearson, Alexander, Sheriff Clerk Depute, County Buildings.

Provan, James, Accountant, 17 Gordon Street.
Raeburn, James, Merchant, 263 Argyle Street.
Ramsay, Thomas, 22 Holyrood Crescent.
Rankin, William, Printer, 192 Argyle Street.
Rattray, John, Plumber, 94 Renfield Street.
Reid, Peter, Dyer, Govan.
Reid, William, Surgeon, 26 Canning Street.
Rice, A. K., Yarn Agent, 51 George Square.
Robertson, John, Engineer, 172 Lancefield Street.
Rochead, J. T., Architect, Wellbridge, Morningside, Edinburgh.
Rodger, George S., Lansdowne Place, Shawlands.
Rodger, William, Parkview, Uddingston.
Ross, A. B., 11 St. Vincent Place.
Ross, William, "Citizen" Office, 34 St. Enoch Square.
Rule, Robert, 13 Ashton Terrace, Dowanhill.
*Salmon, James, I.A., 197 St. Vincent Street.
Salmon, W. Forrest, I.A., 197 St. Vincent Street.
Scotland, J., Custom House.
Scott, Bailie, 32 Jamaica Street.
Scott, Thomas, 6 Queen's Square, Strathbungo.
Scott, William, 18 Old Broad Street, London.
Service, James, Writer, 35 Bath Street.
Shand, George, Chemist, Stirling.
Simpson, John, Muirpark, Renfrew.
Smellie, T. D., Surveyor and Valuator, 213 St. Vincent Street.
*Smith, Gordon, Writer, 133 West George Street.
Smith, James, Benvue, Dowanhill Gardens.
Smith, Robert, Wine Merchant, 124 Sauchiehall Street.
Somerville, Rev. Thomas, 5 Richmond Street.
Stark, Andrew, 41 Queen Street.
Steel, James, Plasterer and Modeller, 25 Holmhead Street.
Stevenson, William, Oil Merchant, 28 Robertson Street.
Stewart, Andrew, Tubemaker, 153 Hill Street, Garnethill.
Stewart, James, 262 Bath Street.
Stewart, John M., Manufacturer, 73 Mitchell Street.

Stewart, Peter, Springfield House, 340 South York Street.
Taylor, James, Druggist, 132 Trongate.
Taylor, William, Surgeon Dentist, 144 Wellington Street.
Taylor, William, 34 St. James's Road.
Templeton, James, Manufacturer, 26B Bothwell Street.
Thomson, Alexander, 6 Nelson Terrace, Hillhead.
Thomson, James, F.G.S., 276 Eglinton Street.
Thomson, James, 25 Monteith Row.
Torrance, William B., Merchant, 55 Hutcheson Street.
Ure, John, Merchant, 68 Washington Street.
Vallance, Alexander, Manufacturer, 62 Queen Street.
Waddell, Alexander, Bank Agent, 44 Canning Street.
Waddell, James, Bank Agent, 419 Gallowgate.
Walker, Andrew, Manufacturer, 23 Royal Exchange Square.
Walker, Robert, Resident Secretary, Reliance Mutual Life
    Assurance Society, 162 St. Vincent Street.
*Watt, Alexander, Writer, 183 St. Vincent Street.
Watt, James, Writer, Airdrie.
Watt, Robert, Writer, Airdrie.
Wellstood, Stephen, Manufacturer, 14 Newington Street,
    Edinburgh.
White, James, Crown Place, Partick.
White, John, Scotstown Mills, Partick.
Whyte, John, Assistant Master of Works, 4 South Albion
    Place.
Whitelaw, Matthew, 37 Queen Street.
Wight, John, C.A., 150 Hope Street, *Honorary Secretary*.
Wilson, Daniel, 87 Hope Street.
Wilson, James, Merchant, 30 John Street.
Wilson, John, South Bantaskine, Falkirk.
Wilson, John, C.A., 59 St. Vincent Street.
Wilson, Thomas M., Warehouseman, 42 Glassford Street.
*Wilson, William, Warehouseman, 42 Glassford Street.
Wink, James, C.A., 4 National Bank Buildings.
Wood, George, Merchant, 27 Frederick Street.
Wylie, Matthew, 239 North Street.

PRINTED BY WILLIAM RANKIN, 192 ARGYLE STREET, GLASGOW.